BLAME IT ON MIDNIGHT

A PARANORMAL WOMEN'S FICTION NOVEL

A MIDNIGHT MADNESS NIGHTCREATURE NOVEL
BOOK TWO

LORI HANDELAND

SOMETHING TO THINK ABOUT

Madison, Wisconsin—Spring 2022

I blame it on midnight. Everything. From the instant the long-lost high school love of my life shifted beneath the midnight moon from a wolf to a man.

Then he bit me.

Yep, I'm a luna werewolf queen now. It was either that or watch my little girl become one. Considering the alpha was her father, that made things complicated.

Story of my life.

But right now I needed to get myself gone from my daughter's apartment bathroom before—

Ding-dong.

That happened.

I was naked, having just showered off what was left of Wendell, the pack's beta, after I ripped him into pieces. Try and kill my girl? I will end your ass faster than you can say *have mercy.*

I peeked out just as the lock clicked open, then the door did too. My daughter, Jenna, who'd been heading in that direction, stepped back when someone stepped in.

Speak of the—

"Alpha." Jenna managed not to glance in my direction.

"You don't have to call me that."

"I'm not callin' you Daddy," Jenna muttered.

Until a few days, ago she'd thought the man she called Daddy was. I'd pointed out that Patrick, my best friend whom I'd married back when I was eighteen, alone and pregnant in nineties small-town Wisconsin, was still her father in every way a father should be.

Except for his being dead, but there was nothing we could do about that.

"Should I call you Gideon Moran?" Jenna continued. "Or maybe Hugh Malik? I'm confused."

Join the club.

The Gideon Moran I'd fallen in love with had been lanky, clumsy, and sweet, a budding computer geek with plain dark-brown hair and plain light-brown eyes.

Hugh Malik, the name Gideon used now, was all muscles and grace, his hair long and black with sapphire highlights, and his eyes shifted from amber to topaz depending on his mood and his form.

It's a werewolf royalty thing.

"You can call me whatever you like," Gideon said.

"What I'd like is for you not to use your hocus-pocus on my door when it's locked."

Qutrubs—the type of werewolves we were—possessed magic, both what we were gifted with at our "birth" and what we killed to take. Gideon could move things with his mind. No idea if that was his innate magic or one of the powers he'd taken. Apparently, it was considered rude to ask.

"I know you're used to doing whatever you—"

"Where's your mother?"

His gaze flicked around the room, and I drew away from the bathroom door, wishing I could disappear myself the way I could magically disappear things, but I couldn't.

While Gideon had become ultra-observant in the twenty-odd years he'd been a werewolf, he didn't have super-duper hearing, smell, or sight. Still, if I wasn't careful, he'd find me. Then, according to werewolf law, once he discovered what I'd done—and he would because Gideon would never let the unexplained absence of his beta go—he'd have to kill me.

"Haven't seen her," Jenna said.

She lied too damn well. Probably because she'd been lying about a helluva lot lately. Practice makes perfect.

"Your mother left me a note saying you had an issue and she was coming here."

"I don't have an issue."

True. I'd killed it.

"Can you call her? My phone's dead."

I nearly fell on my face diving for my jeans where my phone would scream my presence when my daughter called me.

I shut it down an instant before she said, "Straight to voice mail."

"I guess I'll wait."

Silence fell. I held my breath.

"I . . . um . . . have to . . ." Jenna headed in my direction.

Unfortunately, my clothes had exploded outward when I shifted, shoes too. All I had in the room was a towel, but beggars couldn't be choosers, so I wrapped it around my body and clutched it to my chest.

Jenna stuck her head in. I put my finger to my lips, and she nodded, then handed over fresh clothes and retraced her steps.

Murmurs commenced, but I didn't try to decipher them. Soon enough, Gideon would come to the conclusion that waiting here was pointless and scout the area. Then he'd find my abandoned car and come right back to search the place. I needed to be gone before either one of those things happened. Luckily, Jenna lived on the first floor, and her bathroom had a window that wasn't painted shut.

I shoved my feet into the sweatpants and sweatshirt, which must have belonged to her roommate since they actually fit—Jenna was not only four inches taller than me but ten pounds lighter. No underwear, no bra. Didn't care. No shoes might be an issue. Even in late-spring Wisconsin, the sky could still spit snow, and the possibility of an overnight freeze, no matter how balmy the day had been, was high. I guess if it came right down to it, I could heal frostbite.

The window slid upward soundlessly; equally soundless, I stepped onto the toilet seat, then over the sill, and onto the ground.

I needed time to figure things out. A place to do it too. Whom could I count on?

In my life there'd been three men I would have trusted *with* my life. One was dead, the other was a werewolf, and the third—

Bingo.

I headed toward where I'd left my Volvo SUV when I'd tumbled out of it as I changed from woman to wolf. The door still hung open, and the keys were in the ignition. I was a little surprised it wasn't gone, considering this was a campus of over forty-five thousand in a city of over two-hundred and seventy thousand. But it was "oh-God-thirty" and a good portion of the students had disappeared to wherever they went for the summer. Still, small favors and all that.

I picked up the tattered remains of my clothes and my shoes from the sidewalk, tossed them into the car, and after a final glance at Jenna's apartment building, I pulled a U-ee and got myself gone.

* * *

I LEFT the city proper and traveled this way, then that. Eventually I remembered to turn on my phone. The voice mail buzzing started right away.

"Fan-fucking-tastic."

For over half my life, I'd been a politician's wife, which had kept my cursing to a minimum. Since Patrick's death, I'd begun to indulge my once-secret hobby of curse-word innovation right out loud. The number of ways I could say *fuck* was amusing as fuckety fuck to me.

The light changed, and the first message played.

"Sarah?"

Gideon's voice after all these years made me start. Sure, it was deeper than it had been at eighteen, there was a growl beneath the surface, but it was him, and I got goose bumps.

"What's going on? Call me back."

God, I had loved him so much. It had broken me when he disappeared. The only thing that had pulled me together enough to go on was our child.

Did I love Gideon still? Did he love me? I thought so. Which was going to be a problem when he found out my secrets.

Message Number Two.

"Your Maj—" Sigh. "Sorry, Luna."

Haley, a girl who'd been kidnapped and turned against her will, was now as stuck in werewolf world as I was. That her great-granddad was the most magnificent werewolf hunter ever born and pretty much everyone in her family was in that biz was a complication for another time.

"Alpha has assigned me to be your omega. That . . . uh . . . means I have your back and I . . . well . . . need to know where that back is. Call me, please. It's . . . um . . . my ass if something happens to you."

Seriously, the pack hierarchy was as confusing as a royal line of succession.

Before I could figure out what to do about Haley, message number three commenced.

"Sunshine?"

I couldn't help it, I smiled at the nickname, which took me

back to a day shortly after Gideon and I had met. *Whenever I look at you, all I see is sunshine on a cloudy day.* Sometimes he'd whistle the tune of the last five words, then kiss my hair. What young woman could resist that?

Not me. Not then. Not now, even though I no longer felt young.

My finger hovered over the telephone icon as I wrestled with the need to call him back, then message number four began to play.

"I can't find Wendell. I had him following Zane. I told you that." Gideon's voice sounded both exasperated and exhausted. I could relate. "Now I can't find Zane either. And I hope you haven't seen him because . . . well, you know."

I did.

Zane was an insanely sexy, gorgeous werewolf problem who spoke with a Haitian Creole accent that trilled along the nerve endings like first love. Once upon a few days ago, Zane had been the beta for a nearby region. Then his alpha had died by werewolf rumble, and he'd become just another minion. I didn't think he liked it.

Beep!

I threw the phone out the window, unsure why I'd started listening to those messages in the first place and belatedly concerned that someone—Gideon—was going to track it, if he hadn't already. I'd buy a burner down the road and call Jenna.

Not long after, I found the country lane that led to where I was going. Several minutes later, the overgrown driveway spit me into a clearing tucked into a deep, dark wood. The place had always given me *Hansel and Gretel* vibes, but now, considering, it felt more *Little Red Riding Hood.*

I cast uneasy glances at the thick, dense trees, which, thanks to my fairy-tale thoughts—curse them!—appeared to heave and hum. Despite the ungodly hour, seemingly every available light fixture blazed within the gorgeous log home.

Why Frankie—my late husband's assistant, a beautiful young man with ridiculously long, dark lashes and very shiny teeth—had built a place that fit him as well as shitkicker boots fit a gazelle had been unclear until I realized he and my husband were a thing. After that, the house made a lot more sense.

Patrick had always wanted a log cabin, the polar opposite of the Victorian family mansion in our hometown of Lunar Lake that he'd been saddled with. I loved that house but Patrick . . . not so much. To him the home was a symbol of all he'd been expected to uphold and all he'd had to hide, and give up, because of it. Yes, being a gay senator might be okay now, but in the Midwest of over twenty years ago, it hadn't been.

Frankie's baby—a peacock-blue 1957 Ford Fairlane convertible—shone beneath the light of the undulating moon, and before I could even knock, the door swung open.

Middle of the night and Frankie matched his car. Smooth. Cool. Classic. His cream trousers held a perfect crease, and his apricot button-down had never known a crinkle. The only indication of the ungodly hour were his bare, narrow feet. We matched.

I lifted my hand. "Hi."

His unwrinkled brow wrinkled. "People have been searching for you."

Old news. The only one who hadn't been, come to think of it, was Frankie. And now that I *did* think of it, and considering . . . everything . . . that was suspect.

"I told them you were visiting a friend."

Oh. Right. I had said that. Had, in fact, pushed him with my mind—my innate werewolf gift—into believing it despite—

"Then someone mentioned you don't have friends."

That.

I had contractors. Suppliers. Consultants. I had made Patrick's Victorian family home into a showplace once featured in *Architectural Digest*, something that had made Patrick proud of the place for the first, and last, time I could recall.

I had neighbors. Fellow members of charitable organizations. Spouses of other politicians. Basically acquaintances. I'd never fit in. Not anywhere. Ever. Except with Patrick. With Gideon. And I hadn't wanted to.

But now would have been a good time to have friends. Someone I could go to for help besides my husband's lover. But you get what you get.

The wind chose that second to rustle through the trees and waft the scent of rotting walnuts across my face. I tensed and whirled, spreading my arms wide, putting myself between that scent and Frankie.

But behind me—to the left and to the right—there was nothing but trees, and when I took another whiff . . . more nothing. Because I'd killed the last werewolf that smelled like that. I knew I had.

"Sarah, what the he—?"

I shoved Frankie inside and slammed the door, flicked the lock, looked for a dead bolt. Didn't find one, but a dead bolt wasn't going to help if a werewolf wanted in. A werewolf would just jump through one of the far too numerous windows.

"Did you ever consider storm shutters for those?"

"To prep for the hurricane that isn't going to hit Wisconsin ever?" Frankie asked.

I started turning off the lights. "Better safe than sorry."

"What are you doing?"

"This place is lit up like Christmas. Anyone out there can see everything in here."

"Why would there be anyone out there? What's going on? Where have you been? Why is everyone so . . . nuts?"

"I'll assume the last question is rhetorical."

Because I'd learned, even before I discovered werewolves, that everyone was nuts in their own nutty way.

Frankie stepped to the picture window, which took up half the front wall, but I yanked the drapes shut so fast he reared back. "Stay away from the windows."

"You're scaring me."

I was, and I felt bad. Coming here was probably the worst choice I could have made. Frankie was an organized, extraordinarily capable, and brilliant political aide. He would be no help in a fight. He didn't own a gun. Even if he did, if *I* did, we would never have thought to buy silver bullets.

A half-laugh, half-sob escaped before I could stop it.

"What is wrong with you?"

So, so much.

"I should go." I stepped toward the door. "This was a mistake. I'm—"

Frankie's phone began to ring. He pulled it out of his back pocket, flicked me a glance. "I gotta . . . it's Gina."

Frankie now worked for Gina Garofolo, the congresswoman running for Patrick's senate seat. And when I say *worked*, I mean *slaved*. Gina was the type of boss who expected 110 percent out of every employee—night, day, weekends, holidays.

Her motto? *Politics never sleeps!*

And the reason for Frankie's being wide-awake and dressed for the day in the dark of night became evident.

"FaceTime. Sheesh." Frankie put a finger to his lips, then turned so "the boss" couldn't see me.

The call connected; Frankie squinted at the screen. "Who the hell are y—?"

"Put Sarah on the phone, please."

Fricking fried fuckscicle!

How had Gideon found me?

A DIVORCE WITHOUT THE PAPERWORK

"I will not put Sarah on!" Frankie's already narrowed eyes narrowed more. "Where's Gina?"

"I have no idea. Sarah. Now."

"Who do you think you are?"

Gideon thought . . . no, he *knew* he was the alpha werewolf king of two werewolf packs, having recently fought to the death to add one to his domain. Sky's the limit when you don't mind tearing out some entrails, then slitting their throat with a silver dagger. But I digress . . .

"It's all right." I beckoned for the phone.

Frankie set the screen against his chest. "Who *is* this asshole?"

"I can hear you," Gideon said.

"I don't care," Frankie returned.

He would if Gideon got really mad and his eyes went topaz, then his face grew fur, a snout, and fangs. I'd like to avoid that.

"I want to talk to my wife." Gideon didn't shout; he didn't have to. The trill of the beast beneath usually got him his way long before any shouting started.

"Your—" Frankie laughed, then he saw my face, and he stopped. "Sarah! He's like twelve!"

Gideon was the same age as I was, but he would look forever eighteen, the age he'd been when he disappeared. And that would have been a problem. Here, there, eventually.

But Wendell in pieces had pretty much been a divorce without the paperwork.

Again, I curved my fingers toward my palm, and after another instant's hesitation, Frankie handed over his phone. I held the screen against my chest the way he had and gave him a look.

"You want me to . . ." He jerked his head to indicate leaving the room.

"If you wouldn't mind."

His scowl said he *did* mind, but he went. Politeness demanded it and Frankie was forever polite.

I waited until I heard a door close, then lifted the phone from my chest. Gideon's familiar face filled the screen.

"How much does he know?" Boxy kitchen cabinets the shade of dying mint leaves—I also enjoyed inventing names for colors that no paint manufacturer would ever consider—filled the frame behind him. Those cabinets revealed Gideon standing within the blue-and-white colonial home he'd purchased in Shipwreck Bay, on the border between his original fifty-mile region and the fifty miles he'd recently "acquired." My fingers literally itched to remodel that mess.

"I haven't told him anything." Though Frankie definitely suspected something, he would never guess *this* something.

"Make sure you don't."

Annoyance flickered. "You might be the alpha, but from what I understand about pack hierarchy, that doesn't make you the boss of me."

Unlike other monarchies, a werewolf pack alpha and luna were pretty much equal.

"Sarah, when humans know what lies beneath, trouble follows. Trust me."

"Jenna knows."

"About that—"

I stiffened. "I am not using magic on my daughter."

"Our daughter."

"Whatever. Not happening."

"It's dangerous for her to know too much."

"I would think it would be more dangerous for her not to know. She needs to be aware, alert, on the lookout for . . . anything, everything. Basically things."

"No one knows she's my daughter."

Unless Wendell had shared.

Had he shared? I didn't even know, for certain, how or when Wendell had found out the truth about my daughter's parentage.

Jenna had said he was good at ferreting out plots and schemes, probably because no one paid much attention to a guy as old and seemingly frail and unassuming as Wendell had been. He could slink around, slip in here, hide behind that, and eavesdrop there. It was as good an explanation as any, and again, he was too dead to ask.

"We should probably still have someone watching her," I said. "Protection. A body guard!"

"I sent someone." Gideon shrugged, and even with a shirt on for a change—werewolves in human form found clothes restrictive, hence my being okay about going commando when I never would have been okay before—I could still see the way his skin seemed to move free of his bones. "Just to be sure."

The enormity of this new world threatened to overwhelm me. Danger around every corner. Uncertainty about whom I should trust. Fear. Lust. Magic. Gideon. The pack. What we needed to do to keep everyone, including Jenna, safe.

"Sunshine?"

My gaze met his, and my insides melted. He loved me. Always had. Probably always would. And because I loved him the same, loved our daughter beyond reason, I had to do what was right. I had to tell him at least one of my truths.

"You need an heir, Gideon, and you aren't going to get one from me."

He said nothing. Must be in shock. I *had* told him, told everyone in fact, that I was on board with producing an heir. I believe my words had been: *Fine. Great. All in.* At the time, I'd have said anything, done anything, to save Jenna.

"I would." Words tumbled from my mouth; I couldn't seem to stop them. "Except I can't. I already went through menopause. Prematurely. Hot flashes. Brain fog." I patted my waistline that wasn't. "This bullshit."

His lips curved, and his eyes softened even more. The expression, the incongruity of it, stopped my babbling even before his words made me gape.

"I know that."

"What? How? Did you hack into my doctor's database?"

As he was standing in Shipwreck Bay, he'd obviously hacked into Gina Garofolo's phone just to get Frankie to answer his call.

Gideon laughed. "Not that I couldn't, but no. Didn't have to."

"Then—"

"I could smell it."

On the heels of "ew!" panic flared. "If you could smell it, then so could—" Everyone in werewolf world.

Except no one had mentioned it, not even Wendell. He'd wanted to turn Jenna, yes. But only because the future, promised heir would be a pup—yep, that's what they called them—and unable to pose enough of a threat to stave off challenges. This contradicted everything Gideon believed—that the mere existence of an heir was a show of strength enough.

Who was right? Who was wrong? Kind of moot.

"Not everyone. Just me. I'm the alpha."

That excuse was getting old.

"If you knew, then how could you—" *I accept—* "Why would you—?"

"You know why."

Because I love you, have always loved you, will never stop *loving you.*

"This is crazy. Dangerous. You need that heir."

"You're my wife," he said. "We'll figure it out."

"I'm not your wife."

"My mate. Same thing."

"You said it wasn't the same. That humans marry and wolves mate."

"Mating is deeper, more." A growl rippled the air. My air, and he wasn't even *in* my air. "Until death, which is a very long time in our world."

I'd allowed this, *embraced* this to save my girl, but now I needed to save not only Gideon, but also the pack that had come to feel like family far too fast.

"I'm sorry, but we need to do whatever we have to do to *undo* this." I waved a finger back and forth between us.

"There is no undoing it."

"I don't believe you." And with that, I disconnected the call, powered down, yanked out the SIM card, and dropped both it and the phone into the tropical fish tank Patrick had given to Frankie one Christmas.

"Sarah! What the hell?" Frankie stood in the entryway from the hall.

"I'll buy you another one."

He waved a hand as if to chase a fly. "Heir? Mates? Pack?"

"You were eavesdropping?" I had waited for the sound of a door closing, but what I hadn't done was check to make sure that Frankie was behind it. Silly me.

"You sound like a lunatic."

"Feel like one too."

Frankie shoved his fingers through his hair, mussing it more than I'd ever seen it mussed. "He's Jenna's dad?"

I nodded.

"Did Patrick know?"

Since Patrick and I had never had sex—surprised he hadn't shared *that* . . . "Of course." I paused, gathering my thoughts. I wasn't supposed to share this, but there was a lot I wasn't supposed to do that I'd already done. "There's another world that lives beneath the moon. One that howls. One that kills."

"You really believe that." It wasn't a question. "What else?"

I told him. All of it. Why not? I could always make him forget.

When I got to the part about Ash, Frankie held up a hand. "The FBI sent a werewolf hunter."

"Apparently, certain cases are routed to them."

"To the . . . what was it? *Jager-Suchers*?"

"Hunter-searchers. When you called your contact and said Jenna was missing, that contact called Ash, who'd been trying to find other missing girls."

His niece, Haley, being one of them.

"I don't know an Ash." Frankie rubbed his temple. "Do I?"

"I made you forget. I didn't want you searching for him or calling anyone who might." And I should have stuck with that plan, but the ship had sailed.

"And where is he now?"

Chained in a dungeon somewhere awaiting execution. I'd tried to find out where but—

"Don't have a clue."

Frankie glanced at the door. "We should probably go."

"Where?"

"Psych hospital."

I laughed so hard I had to bend over to catch my breath.

"You finished?" he asked when I had. "Were you experimenting with psychedelics? Weird mushrooms? Bad food? Did someone slip you a mickey?"

"I don't think that's what they call it anymore." Though what they called it I had no idea. "You believe I'm crazy."

"As a shithouse rat. No offense."

I snorted; I'd heard worse on the campaign trail. "And Gideon?"

"Who's Gideon?"

"Guy on your phone."

"Ah. The alpha." He twisted the title into an insult, and annoyance trilled along my spine. "Shared delusion?"

"What about these?" I pointed at my formerly gingham-blue eyes, now a lovely royal cerulean.

He frowned; he hadn't noticed them. Maybe because I had turned off all the lights.

"Tinted contacts."

Except I wasn't wearing any, but why bother? He was going to see what he wanted to see, it was the way of humans when what they saw was impossible.

I strode for the door.

Frankie hurried to keep up. "I'll call ahead, talk to someone I know at the—" He peered into the fish tank, where all the pretty fishies flitted around his phone like it was a brand-new fish toy. "Crap."

"Guess it's show-and-tell time," I said. "Or maybe tell, then show."

Why I didn't just zap his memory—again—I wasn't sure. Perhaps a nagging concern that doing so too many times might give him a brain bleed. Or maybe I just needed someone to know. Someone who wasn't part of this frightening new world I'd been thrust into. Still, telling Frankie had been a dumb idea. All about what I needed, what I wanted. Selfish.

"Hold on. Let me . . ." He glanced around, lost as a millennial without a cell phone. Or a landline.

I set my hand on the doorknob. "Don't worry. I won't tear out your throat." I yanked open the door.

The wolf on the porch lifted his lip, and a snarl curled free.

"But he might."

STAY HERE AND MEET THE T. REX

The wind ruffled the wolf's shimmering bronze fur; eyes the shade of the Pacific blazed. He attempted to stalk into the house, and I stepped in front of him; he snapped at me.

"Jesus, Sarah, get away from that thing!"

Frankie's shout drew Zane's attention, and I swore the little fucker smiled; his fangs dripped saliva. Then, between one blink and the next, the wolf became a naked man.

Zane naked was a beautiful thing. I took an instant to enjoy it because I knew when he spoke, I'd only want to kill him again.

Tall and slim with abs so chiseled they appeared painted on his dusky, perfect skin; the muscles in his arms and legs slid beneath that skin in a way that tantalized. I became distracted, as women—probably men too—did around Zane, and he slipped past me and into the room.

Zane gave Frankie the once-over, and his gaze lingered. When he saw me notice, he gave the Gallic shrug that was as much a part of him as his burnished-copper waterfall of tangled, curly hair. The type of hair that made you want to shove your fingers into it for any number of reasons, most of them carnal, some homicidal.

"Centuries are long, *mon amie*."

Zane peppered his Haitian Creole with enough French that it had made me wonder if he'd spent a few years at the court of Louis the something or other in the eons since he'd supposedly been birthed in Haiti.

"Boredom sets in, and I am weak."

"You aren't weak, and I am not your friend." I wanted to add "dick," but I shouldn't poke the bear. Wolf. Man. Wolf-man? "How did you find me?"

"Were you hiding?"

Apparently not very well.

"He-he-he was a wolf."

I'd forgotten Frankie. He'd been so quiet. Also, you didn't turn your back on Zane. Not if you wanted to keep a knife out of it. Instead, I inched next to, but slightly in front of, Frankie, keeping my eyes on the newest threat.

"And then he—" Frankie paused to hyperventilate. I should probably grab him a paper bag, but . . . Zane.

Instead, I touched my forehead and whispered, "It's fine, Frankie. Hush."

And Frankie said, "It's fine," then he hushed.

"Interesting." Zane's too-beautiful-for-such-a-PITA gaze pinned me.

Crap. He hadn't known I could push people. Guess that cat was out of the bag. Maybe I could push him later to forget all about it.

I took Frankie's hand and squeezed it once. He squeezed back, and after a quick glance at his face, which was whiter than I liked but less gray-green than it had been, I released him and focused on the problem in front of us. "What do you want, Zane?"

"You."

I lifted an eyebrow. "In hell."

His smile gave me a tingle I didn't much like. "That can be arranged."

Bravado was called for. Fake it till you make it.

I stepped in close, a move meant to intimidate. Even though Zane probably had six inches on me, I was still his queen. "Why have you come?"

"To help you. You are my luna after all."

Though I'd just had the same thought, I wasn't buying it coming from him.

"And why do I need help?"

He lifted a single eyebrow the shade of ancient rust. "You know why."

Zane had seen me obliterate Wendell. It was one of the reasons I'd run. I doubted he'd keep quiet for long. Or if he did, he'd want something. What was it?

"You're going to have to spell things out."

Zane glanced at Frankie, and I waved my hand. "Don't worry about him. He knows the score."

Frankie hadn't believed me, but I thought he might now.

"The *Book of Books* forbids sharing our truth with the common man."

"Whoops," I deadpanned.

This *Books of Books*, a werewolf Bible, was really getting on my nerves. Especially since I'd never seen it, hadn't read it. How was I supposed to know this shit?

"I've already broken a cardinal rule, so . . ." I spread my hands.

Zane's smile widened. "You killed a werewolf outside of a challenge fought in a ring."

"And the punishment for that is death. Move on."

"Sarah!" Frankie whispered, horrified, but I didn't have time to soothe him. I didn't have time to soothe myself.

"Alpha is on his way."

I wondered how Gideon knew where I was, how Zane had, despite my pathetic precautions to the contrary, then decided it didn't matter, because they did. I edged toward the door.

"He will find you."

"You seem inordinately pleased by that. Should I assume you already tattled?"

"*Moi?*" Zane set a long-fingered, clever hand against his buff, gleaming pecs. "*Mais non!*"

I rolled my eyes.

Zane laughed. He seemed to find me amusing. Perhaps he just liked to torture puppies until they rolled over and presented their fat, sweet little bellies for a final cut; anything so he would stop, stop, stop!

"As I said before, I have come to help, to spirit you away to a place where you will be safe, where Alpha cannot find you. No one knows about your transgression but *moi et toi*." He smirked. "Me and you."

"Got it." But did I believe it? It would be smart for him to tell someone else, at least put the information somewhere safe, just in case, because . . . "What's to keep me from eviscerating you the instant we're away from prying eyes?"

"Sarah!" Frankie said again.

Again, I ignored him. This was who I was now, and he was going to have to accept it, accept me, or . . . I wasn't sure.

"I trust you, *Ou Majesté*."

"You don't trust me any more than I trust you."

"*C'est vrai*."

I assumed that meant something along the lines of *true*, but I didn't ask. Places to go, people to avoid.

"I think I'll take my chances on my own."

Zane lowered his voice as I passed him on the way to the door. "If you do not come with me, I will tattle, as you say."

"Like Gideon's going to believe anything you say."

"Perhaps so, but the photographs"—he kissed the tips of his fingers, then tossed them upward—"*la perfection*."

"But on film we're shadows." I'd seen the wisps and whirls that slunk and slithered, never materializing into anything solid, in the security video the night of Jenna's supposed disappearance.

"*Oui,*" he agreed. "Unless one involves magic."

I was so damn over magic. And who'd have thought that would happen? I mean *magic*, it's cool, right?

Not always.

"This evidence has been placed somewhere safe, with someone I trust, and if I meet a mysterious demise, it will be sent to Alpha post haste. Once he sees these photos, then you will die, and Alpha will mourn. I do not think he will get over you as quickly as he got over the other."

"Other" being Gideon's mate before me. The one Ash swore he had not killed, even though everyone believed that he had. But my money was on this guy.

I filed that suspicion away to take out again when I might have time to dig into exactly what Zane had been up to in the past—if I survived that long.

"Why do you want to help me?" I made finger quotes around "help" because I knew this help would most likely be unhelpful in the long run.

Zane bowed so low my back hurt, then opened the door, sweeping his lithely muscled arm out in an elaborate "be my guest" gesture before he straightened and eyes the shade of an endless sea captured mine.

"I will hide you from Alpha until the storm you have created passes, until you are safe from execution, then I will keep your secret until the end of time."

I resisted the urge to roll my eyes again. Around Zane, I always wanted to. "And in return?"

Despite his being too far away for such a thing, I felt his whisper stir my hair. "In return, I desire a luna favor."

He'd tried to extort a favor from me at the murder sight, offered to scorch Wendell's bones into oblivion—shooting flame from his fingers being one of his magical powers. I wasn't sure of the others. I thought a lot of people weren't, including Gideon. Luckily, I'd discovered before I'd agreed that I could disappear things on my own. Unfortunately, Wendell's magic only worked with inanimate objects, or I'd have disappeared Zane on the spot.

"What's a luna favor?"

"A favor from the luna."

I managed, barely, to keep from saying *no shit*.

"Which I may claim whenever I like."

I didn't care for the idea of granting an unnamed favor at an unnamed time, but he was right about my needing a place to go that no one knew about. I never should have put Frankie in the line of fire, but I'd never been in a line of fire before.

A howl started up in the distance, lifting toward the descending moon.

"Tick, tock, my queen. He is coming."

The howl became louder and louder, seeming to swirl through the open doorway. Frankie put his hands over his ears, closed his eyes, and shouted, "Make it stop!"

"Do you agree to my terms?"

"Fine. Yes. Whatever." I could renege later. Deny, deny, deny. No one had heard me agree, and I was the queen. While Zane had once been a beta, he'd arrived here as a sigma, a lone wolf, and he pretty much was again. Who would the pack believe?

This thought was unlike me; I knew it even as I thought it. Then again, I was not me, or at least not the me I'd been last week.

Zane's triumph was disgusting to behold. I wanted to punch him, but I didn't have time.

I pulled one of Frankie's hands away from an ear, then leaned in close, using my other hand to touch my forehead. "You can't hear the howl, Frankie." He dropped both hands, and I leaned back. "You have no idea where I went."

I followed Zane onto the porch and closed the door as Frankie used a net to fish his phone out of the fish tank.

The howl stopped; my ears rang with the silence. I started toward the car, and Zane said, "*Non*!"

I rounded on him. "You said we needed to hurry."

"Not in the automobile."

"He won't be able to catch us if we drive."

Yes, we were werewolves, and magic ones to boot, but beneath the magic, when we were wolves, we were wolves, faster than humans but not as fast as a car.

Zane headed for the trees, his lack of concern for things that were, to me, quite concerning made my eye twitch. I tried to swallow the burn of annoyance that threatened to rumble free of my chest and straight out my mouth in a snarl. Then decided *why swallow it* and let the sound burst free.

Zane let out a huff. Good. I shouldn't be the only one with an eye twitch.

"Where we are going an automobile cannot, and if you do not want His Majesty to catch us, you need to—" He threw his arms theatrically into the air and shifted in the space of a blink, then strolled into the midnight shadows created by the trees.

Zane's wearing ears and a tail made it easier for me to strip. Sure, he leered, just to be an ass; he definitely wasn't interested in this post-menopausal body. Though when I glanced down, I decided that from this angle I didn't look all that bad.

No more full-length mirrors. I would make it a rule. It was good to be the queen.

The first time I'd shifted, there'd been pain. Being reborn hurt, it cut; I had throbbed and burned and ached. But apparently becoming a wolf was like becoming a woman. It only smarted the first time. Since then, shifting had been glorious.

The initial change had also seemed to take an eternity. However, while I was too new a wolf to shift as Zane did—blink, he's a wolf—I could do so much faster than an eternity.

I reached for my wolf, and in a smooth, wheeling twirl, the magic unfurled. She was there; she was me.

As a wolf, I was a beauty. Platinum fur, aquamarine eyes, lithe and sleek and strong.

At first, I'd also been vicious. Then Gideon had nose-bumped me—magic he'd taken from another in the ring—and the mindless anger and fury had been gone. I'd believed the desire to rip and shred and kill anything in my path had disappeared forever. Then someone had touched my little girl.

Now I was on the run. With the wolf least likely to be elected follower of the month.

Power rushed in my veins, and I accelerated to catch up to Zane, who'd taken off as if hell were on his heels. Perhaps it was.

Zane seemed to think that we could outrun, or at least outmaneuver, Gideon. I didn't trust him, not really, but if Zane planned to feed me to the big bad wolf, he'd have done so already. Sure, he was up to something; I just wasn't sure what. But if I found out, perhaps I could use that to gain my way back into Gideon's good graces.

Palace intrigue at its finest.

The forest shimmered—silver, purple, silvery-purple—a sheen so startling, so strange I put on the brakes, and my claws dug furrows in the hard-packed dirt.

Zane stopped too, then tossed his head to indicate a small break in the thick tree canopy. Shit. The sun was coming up. When it touched us, we would change in a blinding flash of light that would alert both the International Space Station and anyone or thing in the vicinity to our presence.

Zane snapped at me, and to avoid a nip that would not only sting my ass but also my pride, I scooted forward. My paw slid into the purply-silver sheet that resembled rain falling from a cloudless sky and disappeared.

I snatched back my paw. Glitter sparkled on my claws as if I'd had a dip powder manicure.

The curtain wobbled. All I caught sight of was the tip of Zane's tail before it was as gone as he was.

A growl rumbled, tickling my ears, making the leaves flutter forward from its origin, reminding me of *Jurassic Park*, the way the earth shook and everything rumbled when a T. rex was coming.

I had two choices: Stay here and meet the T. rex? Or step into the unknown?

WAS I REALLY KIDNAPPED?

The forest on the other side of the iridescent curtain appeared exactly the same. The only indication that we had exited one world and entered another was the shiny silver and purple flecks that twinkled on both Zane's and my fur.

It tickled, and I shook. Starlight fluttered to the ground as a great, black beast, his silky coat glistening with threads of sapphire, emerged from the foliage we had left behind.

He stood impossibly still, his topaz gaze flickering left, right, ahead. He seemed to stare right at me, his snout so close to mine I took a step back, tangling my legs—four not two, Sarah!—and nearly kissing dirt.

Zane cast me a disdainful glance, which made me consider tearing out his throat, before he returned his attention to Gideon and smirked. As much as a wolf can smirk.

Gideon stalked into the trees. Light flashed an instant before he shouted, "Sarah!"

My heart clutched; my stomach clenched. I wanted to go to him, but I couldn't. Or at least I wouldn't. Yet. I needed to figure out my shit before I made another move.

I didn't trust Zane. Did anyone? But I did believe he wanted something from me—that luna favor—and he'd do what he'd promised in order to get it. If he didn't . . . well, I'd deal with that when it happened. Right now, I was putting out fires as they happened.

The sun sifted over Zane, over me, and we shifted.

"What *is* that?" I threw out my arm to indicate the curtain of splendor.

Zane shook the sparkles from his hair; they fluttered onto his shoulders, his pecs, highlighting their perfection before melting away.

Zane offered his arm; I turned up my nose. I wasn't so easy with the naked that I planned to touch him. I also wasn't so old that I needed help.

He sighed—I'm sure I was a great trail—then strode ahead. "I told you I am different from the others."

He hadn't had to tell me. One look, a single word, and I knew.

As mentioned, Gideon's pack, and the pack he had taken as his own, were *Qutrubs*—born of a demon, a.k.a. a wolf, and a jinn in the heat of the Middle Eastern deserts—Zane was not.

I fell in step beside him. "You're a loup-garou."

"Born of a mambo—"

Priestess. Sorceress, my mind whispered.

"—and a wolf. Because of this I can cast spells."

"Get out!"

He threw me a confused glance, and I had to remind myself that even though he lived in this, a modern world, he had been conceived, lived, perhaps died in another, and slang seemed to elude him. Or he pretended it did.

"No kidding?" His brow creased deeper, so I tried, "Wow!"

"Ah. Yes. Once I discovered that I could make magic if only I practiced enough, life became, as you say, 'wow.'"

We began to climb a hill where the trees grew so closely together we could not pass through two abreast and had to follow single file. No wonder Zane had nixed the use of my car.

I wasn't panting; I hadn't yet broken a sweat, and as I didn't own a StairMaster, and wouldn't have used one if I did, I was impressed with my stamina.

"When did you discover this magic? After you were turned?"

"I did not turn. I have always been what I am."

"Wait. What? You were a baby and you—"

"I was not a baby."

"You came out like . . ." I slid a hand up and down to indicate his bare feet, his *don't hate me because I'm beautiful* hair and all that lay in between.

"*Non*. A loup-garou can procreate same as the *Qutrub*."

Other werewolf species could not, most couldn't even touch without getting an extreme ice-cream headache. Which might be why Zane had been accepted into a tribe that wasn't, technically, his own.

"Or the same as the *Qutrub* before the *maladie*."

There'd been a virus. The females had died. A cure had given them hope. Trafficking had brought them new blood.

Gideon had been able to put a stop to the kidnapping and forcible changing of human females into werewolf mates because our daughter, and her mad scientist vet school adviser, had cured the "maladie." They were still short females, but in Gideon's pack, from now on, only those who agreed to be changed—for whatever reason—would be.

"I was an infant," Zane continued, "but also a pup."

"You shape-shifted when you were still in diapers?" That had to have been a treat.

"When I was in the womb."

Even better.

"I drove my *manman* . . ."

My head tilted at the slight shift in the French *maman* to what must be the Haitian Creole *manman*.

"*Modi*! I drove my *manman* . . . what is the word?"

He knew the word. And because he did, and I knew that he

did, and he probably knew that I knew that he did, I smiled sweetly and murmured, "Batshit?"

He twitched one perfect shoulder; he was very hard to rile. "We are what we are, and so I was this. I am this."

"How many times did you set fire to your nursery when you . . .?" I waved at his fingers.

"*Cette*?" He shot flames from those fingertips, making a nearby tree into a conflagration.

I had a mental flash of a YouTube video I'd seen of a forest fire, before he flicked his other hand, and rain poured out of nowhere, and the fire went out with a hiss. Hadn't known he could do that.

"*Pa janm*. Not ever. My powers are from spells and not innate."

"All of them?"

"*Oui*."

This explained why the curtain had shielded us from Gideon. Wolf magic did not work on a pack member's luna or alpha, which meant a spell was not wolf magic per se.

"Can you or can you not take a werewolf's power by killing them?"

"I am not an alpha, and only alphas are allowed to kill, and only in a ring."

Not an answer. I wasn't shocked. Zane excelled at the nonanswer answer.

"I'm not an alpha. I didn't take Wendell's power in the ring. Yet I have it."

"You are not, and yet you did," he agreed. "Which is why you are here. With me."

"Do you ever give anyone a straight answer?"

"Not if I can help it."

We reached the top of the seemingly endless hill—I still wasn't panting, yay me!—and I started to descend the other side. A warm breeze caressed my neck, then curled over my collarbone, and circled one breast. The nipple peaked so fast and so hard I gasped.

Pain? Pleasure? Both?

I crossed my arms over myself. "How much far—?"

No sign of Zane, but the dark circlet of a cave entrance loomed in the bright light of dawn. Was he in there? Where else could he be?

I approached cautiously. One thing rural Wisconsin youngsters learn is to never crawl into a hole in the earth. This wasn't called the Badger State because badgers were cute. Badgers were mean as fuck and spoiling for a fight twenty-four seven.

I hunkered down. "Zane?"

Nothing stirred but the wind.

I duckwalked closer, and a hand reached out, then yanked me inside.

My gasp was a shriek, or at least it seemed that way to me. In reality, the only sound was the *thunk* of my face kissing dirt when I overbalanced.

I lifted my head, no longer expecting a badger or a bear—they didn't have hands—but

definitely *not* expecting the unfurling of a gold-flecked white robe in front of my face. It looked like something that might have been worn by the last queen of Pompeii. But naked women couldn't be choosers, so I threw the robe over my head. The garment caressed my skin as the wind had. My nipples poked at the bodice like a pebble poked at the sand.

I crossed my arms again and took stock of my surroundings.

Once through the low entrance, the cave widened, broadened, heightened into a cavern. The air was significantly chillier within than without; the scent reminded me of the dust that filtered through open windows when driving a car too fast on gravel roads.

The only explanation for the light that pulsed from the walls themselves was magic, yet several passages that led deeper into the hill loomed as dark as a yawning grave beneath the new moon.

Zane dipped his head. "Welcome to my lair."

Lair sounded so ridiculous I gave a Bronx cheer. Gideon had also used the word to describe his king suite at the abandoned warehouse castle. Must be a werewolf thing. There were a lot of them.

"You asked me to take you where he would not find you."

"I believe you offered."

His teeth flashed. They seemed far too white to be a gazillion years old. "For a price, *Ou Majesté.*"

"A luna favor."

"What will it be?" He tapped his luscious lips with a supple finger, and something deep inside my girl parts fluttered.

"Can you put on some clothes?"

Zane glanced down as if he'd forgotten he wore none. I suppose that could happen. More than likely he just enjoyed airing his man bits. For man bits, they weren't half bad. The issue was, he knew it.

Arrogant men, not my thing, though Gideon was far more arrogant as a werewolf king than he'd ever been as a sweet, geeky young man. He had to be.

I tried some arrogance of my own, snapping the flowing skirt of my robe at the same time I snapped, "Clothes."

Amusement caused Zane's gaze to sparkle like bright sun atop tropical waters; he clapped his hands, and something swirled in the gloom that shrouded the nearest passageway; air rolled across the ground; tiny whirls of dirt drifted across my toes.

A man materialized from the darkness. The light-brown peach fuzz on his cheeks and chin made him appear fourteen years old, though he could be fourteen hundred for all I knew. His hair stuck out every which way as if it really were the straw its shade suggested.

I'd seen him among Badru's wolves, part of the pack Gideon

had taken, or at least the pack he *thought* he'd taken, which made the kid's presence here suspect. He offered Zane the jeans he'd brought from . . .

I stepped closer to the passageway, but the light from the cavern only spread a few feet and beyond that, who knew?

Zane zipped the jeans, managing to look sexier in them than out of them with the button gaping to reveal a disappearing happy trail. No shirt, no shoes, but with shapeshift-rumpled hair he could probably get any kind of service, anywhere that he wanted.

"Where do those lead?" I jabbed a finger at the murky doorway.

"Wherever I wish."

I let out an annoyed burst of air. "Where did this guy come from?"

Said guy stood at attention, eyes front. Robo-wolf. I'd encountered them before.

"His *manman*."

My eye started to twitch again. "Why is he here?"

"You ordered me to put on clothes, and as you can see, he has brought clothes."

"Why didn't you just magic yourself some?"

"I magicked him."

I refrained from rolling my eyes, barely. "I don't consider going commando in jeans to be clothes, but that's not the point."

Zane's brow furrowed, and he opened his mouth, no doubt to pretend he did not know what *commando* meant, and I held up a hand. "What. Is. This. Place?" I held up my other hand to forestall more mind-blowing double-talk. "Besides your lair? Complete with minions, secret passageways, and . . ." Now I threw up my arms. "I don't know what else."

"You will." Zane tossed his hand, and the wolf-kid ducked into the hall he had ducked out of and disappeared into the dark as if he'd fallen off a cliff.

My patience was gone. I had been holding back on my magic, a bit afraid that using my brain-pushing power would blow the minds of those I used it on, but if I was going to test-dummy the power on anyone, I wanted to test it on Zane. He was making me so crazy I'd begun to worry about blowing a few of my own remaining brain cells.

I touched my forehead. "Where am I?"

I felt a strange sensation, like a shove in my brain.

I tried again. "Where do those passages lead?"

Another sharp brain shove, then I blinked like an owl in the sunlight when, instead of the truth pouring from Zane's mouth, laughter did. No one but Gideon had ever resisted my magic.

Zane took my hand—so gently it freaked me out. At least he'd stopped laughing.

"This is my world. Your magic does not work here."

I looked around for something, anything, to make disappear. All I had were various rocks, so I picked up one, and I wished it gone.

Nothing happened.

I reached for my wolf. She wasn't there either.

"If my magic doesn't work here, I think I will be going."

"Out into the world where you are a murderer, a fugitive?"

"Yes."

"*Soit mon invité.*" He swept out his hand. "Be my guest."

I'd have crawled out of the exit I'd come in. If it were still there.

My hands curled into fists, and a shriek of fury exploded, bouncing off the walls of the cave, then echoing down the endless halls.

I gathered myself, calmed myself. "I am your luna. You pledged your allegiance. You must do as I say." I waited a beat. "Right?"

"*Oui,*" he said at last. "You asked me to hide you, to shield you from harm. This I am doing. This I *will* do."

"Even if I wish to go?"

"Even if." He headed for the nearest passage.

Had Zane just kidnapped me? Had I let him? If I'd let him, was I really kidnapped?

What purpose could he have for doing that?

Zane paused in the entryway of a hall that now pulsed with light and beckoned.

Did I want to go in there with Zane? No. Did I want to stay in a dark cavern alone perhaps until the end of time?

Also no.

THE ONLY WAY OUT —MAYBE—WAS IN

I followed Zane into a passageway that rolled out ahead of us, a carpet made of dirt and stone. I didn't want to follow, but I was stuck.

The only way out—maybe—was in.

Another arched doorway appeared to our right, and Zane indicated I should precede him. As the room, passage, prison cell, cliff's edge was shrouded in a darkness so deep it appeared infinite, I held back. "No, thank you."

He took a step in my direction, and for an instant I thought he planned to toss me through. Then he gathered himself and dipped his head in his snooty version of deference before he flipped his hand skyward like a Vegas magician, and the room lit up so bright I had to close my eyes.

"Yikes! My corneas!"

The light beyond my closed lids toned down a few laser watts, and I slowly opened them. The room was stunning. Everything I'd ever wanted to put into the Sullivan Victorian family home and hadn't, either because I couldn't find it or couldn't condone the astronomical cost, was there.

Before I realized what I was doing, I'd stepped in and laid my hand on the Chippendale sofa. The mahogany gleamed, unscathed, as if it hadn't been touched by a sharp instrument since its inception.

I circled the piece. Camelback. Claw and ball feet. A tinge of dried carnation to the brocade. Not a stain in sight. My fingers itched to search for one, but the ridge of dirt beneath nails that had once been claws stopped me.

I'd considered buying a Chippendale back in the day but balked at the price tag. That piece had been nicked, scratched, stained. If this one ever had been—and as it was easily over two centuries old, it *had* to have been—the restoration was exquisite. Price over eighty grand.

But the hand-knotted rug the shade of two-week-old dried mud was the real prize. Those things could go for hundreds of thousands. My brain silently tallied the walnut bed, the armoire, the nightstands.

"This room cost more than my house."

Zane shrugged. Living forever, barring an unfortunate piercing with silver, did wonders for the bank account. "You approve?"

I wasn't sure. Except for the cave walls, on which it would no doubt be near impossible to install the flowered wallpaper common to a Victorian-era bedroom restoration, even if the freaky glowing rock didn't melt the glue, it was perfect. It was all I'd imagined a Victorian bedroom to be back when I'd been reimagining one, and I couldn't help but walk around touching things some more. The elaborate rococo-style carving gracing the nightstands was flawless.

Restoring the house had once been my salvation. My sanity. Something to focus on besides Gideon's whereabouts. Because when I thought about that, I imagined terrible things.

He was dead in a ditch.

He was captive on a ship to Botswana.

He was buried in a shallow grave.

He was chained in a serial killer's basement.

Anything but that he'd left me on purpose.

His becoming a werewolf . . . hadn't crossed my mind.

"I wanted you to have what you had dreamed."

Zane's sinuous, mesmerizing voice intruded on my thoughts, and I was glad. My thoughts these days, while more focused than they'd been during the brain fog of menopause, were nevertheless anything but clear.

"I hoped this would make your stay here most pleasant."

"But . . . how did you know? When did you . . .? It would have taken years to find all this and—"

Zane lifted his hand to his heart. "You wound me, *Ou Majesté*. For you to think that I could not create your heart's desire." He whirled his hand like a magician, and I got it.

A spell had conjured my heart's desire. What else had he, could he, would he conjure?

A sudden longing to be gone from this room overwhelmed me, and I hurried for the hall.

I reached the doorway, and I could not step any farther. My feet would not listen to my brain. I lifted my hand, tried to put it through whatever magic Zane had made, but I couldn't. My palm stopped on my side of the barrier, and the air between us shimmied, making me dizzy. "What have you done?"

"I am keeping you safe."

"In a gilded cage?" The flawless bedroom suddenly made a lot more sense. "I want out of here."

"As soon as you pay your luna favor, the barrier will be gone."

"If Gideon finds out what you've done, he'll kill you."

Zane tilted his head. "If he finds out what you've done, he'll kill you."

Stalemate.

"What is it you want for your luna favor?"

"You."

I threw out my arms. "You got me."

"Not your mere physical presence." He looked me up and down, his gaze seeming to penetrate my robe and where that gaze had been scornful when we'd met, now it was anything but. "Your body, in my bed. My body, in yours."

I laughed. He did not, and my laughter died.

"Let me get this straight, you—who sneered when Gideon chose me—are now choosing me?"

"You agreed to give me a luna favor in exchange for protection. A luna favor *is* sex."

That wasn't what he'd said. Though what *had* he said? The favor was whatever he wished for it to be. I hadn't done a deep dive on that, and I should have.

"How can you ask this?"

"I am not asking."

I stilled. "You plan to take it?"

Take me was left unsaid.

"*Mais non*. I would never. I *have* never. Women's bodies, and men's as well, have always been freely given."

"Not mine."

"We shall see."

He knew something I didn't, again. I hated it. Hated him.

"You pledged your allegiance to Gideon."

"I did not."

I gaped. "I was there. You did."

"I may have pledged . . ." His lips curved with the sly little secret he couldn't wait to share. "But he never acknowledged it, and therefore it does not bind me."

I thought back. The pack had knelt, one by one, after each expression of loyalty we had given a regal head bop.

Zane had knelt in front of me—pledge, head bop—he had pledged to Gideon and then . . .

There'd been snarls and growls and yips as a skirmish broke out between Badru's wolves and Gideon's. Gideon had intervened. Before he'd acknowledged Zane's pledge. I'd thought the nod merely ceremony, now . . .

"You caused that skirmish, didn't you?"

"How could I possibly? I am not an alpha; I am no longer even a beta. I am nothing. No one. I have no power over any wolves."

I didn't believe him. That skirmish had been far too convenient.

But if Zane had orchestrated it, I had to wonder . . . Were Badru's wolves really Gideon's, or were they his?

I smelled *coup* all over this.

"I am *not* going to sleep with you."

"Then a gilded cage it is." He strolled into one of the passageways and was gone, at least from my sight.

I sat in that cage all day. When my stomach growled, food appeared, all of my favorites—bacon, hashbrowns, pancakes, lasagna, garlic bread, German chocolate cake. Things I hadn't allowed myself to eat in years, and I stuffed them all into my face.

Why not? If this asshole didn't kill me, Gideon would.

I wished for clothes, but none appeared. Because Zane didn't wish for me to have them considering what he wanted from me or because deep down I preferred the satiny robe brushing my skin? Hard to say. Bottom line: I guess I should be happy I had a robe.

The heavy meals, along with a lot of red wine—also, why not? —had my eyelids drooping soon after. I pulled back the vintage-white comforter decorated with cabbage roses the shade of a newly dead salmon from the bed, then crawled in. At least they smelled of lavender and not fish.

I awoke in the dark, and I thought I was home. With Gideon. In Shipwreck Bay. We'd had one night there—a beautiful, wonderful night where we'd consummated a love we'd both thought gone.

One night and the place was home. Or maybe he was.

Then I caught the scent of lavender, and I remembered—

Zane, the cave, the bedroom of perfection, my captivity, and the terms of my release.

I considered the impenetrable blackness surrounding me. Something wasn't right.

There hadn't been any darkness when I fell asleep, instead the light had continued to pulse eerily from the stones. I'd figured it always would. Wasn't that how they broke POWs, making them live in the light, never allowing them sleep? I was surprised Zane hadn't started playing Metallica at a head-banging volume or sprayed me with a fire hose.

I decided to enjoy it while I could. With rest, food, and water I could outlast this jerk. And when he realized that, the "guest" treatment would end. Then I'd need to hold on until someone found me.

Would someone find me? Could they?

I drifted in a world of lavender and feather pillows, not asleep but not completely awake. And in that netherworld my body remembered the accidental brush of Gideon's fingers against my wrist the first time he'd walked me home. I had felt that touch so deep I'd gasped, and he'd said—

"Sorry! I didn't mean—"

I grabbed his hand; I held it tight. I never wanted to let it go.

"I do. Mean this." I squeezed, and then I tried something I'd only read about. I ran my fingernail across his palm, and he—

Gasped. The sound, me not him, brought me back to a place I did not want to be.

Cave. Cell. Kidnapped. Scared. Alone.

I tumbled back into the dream.

We'd been seeing each other for weeks. Not dating, not really. Gideon had no money for movies or hamburgers—he didn't have money for a soda—and he wouldn't let me pay with mine. But as long as I was with him, nothing else mattered.

My parents had taken one look at his shoes, which had as many holes as his jeans, then frowned at the hair his mom hacked off every once in a while, leaving it both short and long, a mess—I didn't care—and pronounced him an unacceptable hoodlum from the wrong side of town who was only after one thing.

They didn't forbid my seeing him; however, if doing so caused too many tongues to wag, they would. I wanted to avoid that. As Lunar Lake was a small town and word traveled, we kept to the woods; we stayed out of sight.

And I wished and hoped and prayed he'd kiss me while the autumn leaves rustled around our feet, and ever so slowly, I burned.

"You don't have to treat me like I'm precious glass, Gideon."

He lifted his hand to my cheek. "But you are. Precious."

Then, at last, his lips touched mine, and the slow burn flamed. Everything, everywhere came alive. My skin pulsed like neon in the night, and I—

Awoke to discover again only the dark, my skin still pulsing on that "almost, almost, yes, yes, please!" edge and vividly reminding me of a long session of kissing that had led to petting, then one touch below my waist, and *kabam*!

I thought that was the way things worked. Later I realized it wasn't, not always, but by then it was too late, and the only one who'd ever made me feel that way was gone.

I could have had an affair—Patrick had—but I'd promised. Or at least that's what I told myself when opportunity arose. To be honest, I was terrified that letting a man touch me would only prove, forever and always, that the only one for me had ever been him. If I didn't try, I couldn't fail. An excuse as old as time.

I tossed and turned until the lights came on. By then I had no idea if I'd been captive hours, minutes, or days. Which was probably the point.

Food and drink continued to materialize. Always exactly what I wanted. I shouted at the door. No one answered. For all I knew, there was no one there. If you could give the prisoner anything without even opening a door that wasn't, why have guards?

A tablet appeared loaded with the book I was currently reading, an online e-zine I favored, the mindless games I played in waiting rooms, along with the streaming service I preferred. How did Zane get Wi-Fi in here? Probably the same way he got the walls to pulse with light.

Gideon could probably hack his way into the tablet and send out an SOS, but Gideon wasn't here, and my tech troubleshooting skills ended at powering down and powering up.

Strange that Zane provided entertainment. Lack of food, water, or sleep wouldn't kill the new me, but boredom might make me cave—ha-ha—faster.

When I thought about it . . . Zane was either really bad at this or he had something up his invisible sleeve that I hadn't figured out.

So I ate and drank and binged on the latest true crime reenactment series, then I fell asleep once more surrounded by the brilliant light. Odd in itself, odder still, the dream.

The forest conveniently rear-ended my house. Both my father and mother worked; my father had his own insurance office, and my mother was the receptionist/office manager. They trusted me. I'd never given them any reason not to.

At first Gideon refused to come inside. But he was an eighteen-year-old boy, and eventually he followed where I led.

I didn't take him to my bedroom. That would have been dumb. Second floor. No exit.

But the basement was exposed, with a sliding glass door that opened six feet from the trees. The floorboards on the first floor creaked whenever anyone walked on them. We'd have plenty of warning and an escape route.

How many times had I wanted to rip off his shirt, do the same with my own, and feel his skin pressed to mine? Now I could, so I did, and it was . . .

My breath rushed out; he captured it with his mouth, murmuring "Sunshine" against my own. When his fingertips brushed my nipples for the first time, I had to bite my lip to keep from moaning.

The basement was cool, but not as cold as the forest, and the slide of my skin against his caused a prickling sensation of heat. Every pore in my body seemed to sizzle, to sing. Then his head lowered, and what he did with his lips, his tongue and teeth . . .

I woke again to the brush of cool air, the echo of that tongue, perched on the sharp, thin edge of fulfillment brought by those teeth.

"Fuck me," I whispered into the dark.

And the lights went on.

A TERRIBLE, BEAUTIFUL MAGIC

"It would be my honor, *Ou Majesté*."

Zane lounged in the doorway. Well, not *in* the doorway, because his damn force field shimmied there, but just outside. Where I couldn't reach.

I shoved my hair—strangely sweaty—from my face. Stranger still . . . my skin prickled like a hot flash was on the way, except I hadn't had a hot flash since . . . I couldn't remember. It was hard to recall the mundane when things just weren't anymore.

"You wouldn't know honor if it bit you on the ass."

"Nevertheless . . ." He shrugged. Still no shirt and his bones slid around beneath his skin in that odd way wolves had. Instead of the jeans from—yesterday? Today? Last Thursday?—he wore loose cotton sleeping pants, which made me think that maybe, possibly it was actually nighttime, but who knew in here. "I am happy to oblige."

My expression must have revealed my confusion.

"You said *fuck me*." Zane's gaze flowed from my face to my neck, then caught on my breasts, and his loose cotton trousers stirred.

"Nope. Not happening." I didn't care to have this conversation while lounging in the bed where I'd just dreamed of Gideon, so I tossed off the covers and stood.

I had been dubbed "hot in her day, but those days are gone" by one of the other pack members. That had stung, as had Zane's blasé dismissal of me as a possible queen. His sudden turnabout was not fair play or in the slightest bit buyable.

"Pretty much nothing you say or do is going to get me to grant you a luna favor."

"Would you like to make a wager?"

I opened my mouth to grant him the favor of my sharp tongue wrapped around several exclusive variations on the F-word, and another tongue brushed mine, teeth tugged at my lip, then that tongue slicked the corner of my mouth.

From ten feet away, Zane's gaze seemed to penetrate my Pompeian robe. Supple fingers danced along my skin, and I shivered, shuddered, and nearly came.

"Have you been enjoying your"—Zane's eyes flicked to the bed and then to mine—"stay?"

I blinked.

"Have I made you feel . . ."

I waited for him to finish that sentence, and when he didn't, understanding dawned.

"It's been you. Making me . . ." Feel. Remember. Nearly, almost come apart. "You cast a spell on me?"

"*Non*. My *manman* cast a spell upon me, allowing me to touch without touching. It has been—" Something came then went across his face. With anyone else I would have labeled the expression sadness, perhaps regret, but this was Zane. "Helpful."

"I bet."

A finger brushed the tip of my nose, then the tip of one breast, another brushed the top of the crack in my ass and slid lower, but Zane stood exactly where he'd been.

"Stop," I said, body on fire.

An endless, avid ocean swirled in his eyes—a terrible, beautiful magic. "It will stop shortly after you consent to let me in."

I started to laugh. I couldn't help it. "You think *not* having an orgasm will make me give in? Loser, I've gone without for decades."

Not precisely true. There were other methods to produce orgasms, something the vibrator industry knew quite well. What they didn't know, or perhaps ignored, was that self-induced took the edge off, but it never quite satisfied that deep-down itch.

"I've found that the longer without"—while his voice, his expression, and his body language all indicated an unearthly calm, a volcano bubbled beneath Zane's surface ocean eyes—"the shorter the time until I am within."

He probably had a point. And if I hadn't found Gideon, known again sex *with* Gideon, sex with love—*making* love—Zane's arrogant prediction might have come true.

But I had, and it wasn't going to.

I crawled under the covers, folded my hands over my stomach, and closed my eyes. I was not, by nature, calm. But I could fake it long enough to drive Jenna bonkers.

Jenna! Crap! I'd snuck out of her apartment and vanished. I'd meant to buy a burner to let her know I was okay, but I'd been a little kidnapped. By now I was sure she'd called Frankie and . . .

Frankie! Crap! With all the crazy going on, I'd loped away without telling him to forget everything werewolf.

Whoops.

But I had used my power to make him believe he didn't know where I was—well, he didn't—so even though he wouldn't try to put Jenna in the same asylum he'd planned to put me, he would be of no help to her.

Before . . . everything, Jenna would have gone to her Uncle Joe—Patrick's brother and the Lunar Lake police chief—but he had no jurisdiction in werewolf land, in werewolf land he'd be toast, and she knew it. She'd have to go to Gideon and tell him . . . well, not the truth—she knew better—but something.

Would she be safe with him? She had to be. There was no one else.

I drifted on the remnants of interrupted sleep and too many thoughts, but trying to ignore Zane was like trying to ignore the tide when it was lapping at your throat. It took concentration, and sometimes concentration induced a trance. That's what meditation was all about. Or so I'd heard.

Behind my eyelids, another memory stirred.

A shaft of sunshine spilled through the sliding glass doors, canting across our naked bodies entwined on the ancient pullout couch covered in the rabid-coyote-gray tweed upholstery that had imprinted tiny polka dots into the skin of my back.

"We can't." Gideon let his forehead drop to mine.

"Don't you want to?" I knew he did. I could feel how much against my stomach. This time the tip of his penis had slipped inside, and I had arched, and we had almost—

"Whoa!" I shot up in bed as fast as a jack-in-the-box shot out of the box.

Zane's eyes, his lips, the slight bulge in his pants told me he knew what I'd dreamed because either he'd caused it, or he could watch it. There was no way I'd zenned myself into that memory without help.

"You're . . . you're . . . Argh!" I threw up my hands; I wanted to tear at my hair. "You're pulling memories from my brain and making them live in my dreams."

"I am?"

My hands curled into fists. I wished, not for the first time, that I had Gideon's power to throttle others from afar. Even if I did, I wouldn't be able to use it in this "no magic for me zone."

"Are they tempting you?"

"No!"

"The night is young."

"And you're old."

He tsked. "Sticks and stones. In my world, being old is power."

"In your world, killing is power."

"Now you are, as they say, 'catching on.'"

There was meaning in that. A threat somewhere, but . . . he'd never tell me.

Zane's head tilted as if he'd heard someone call. "Your answer is no?"

I gave him the finger.

He wolf-shrugged. "I will return every night until you agree." Then he was gone, down one of the endless hallways that led, I hoped, to hell.

The next night, I tried to stay awake, should have been able to considering I did nothing all day but laze around. Though I'd found, in the past, that the less I did, the more tired I became, and while I had a very good reason not to let my eyes close, I could not keep them open.

"Please," I whispered.

"We need to stop."

I shook my head, trying to think of a word other than please, *but the air, the world, this room, my life had narrowed to only that, this, him.*

I held Gideon against me. I wouldn't let him go. I would never *let him go. I wanted him to be my first. "Please. Now. Please."*

He rolled to the side, and I cried out, but he touched me then, right where I hadn't known I needed him to, and it was, it was—

"Magic," I said into the darkness, my body perched again on the precipice.

The rasp of my breathing was loud in the chill of the night. My hair was damp, same as before. I was damp.

"I can make you beg." Zane's whisper swirled into the blue-black nothing. "I can make you scream."

"You're drugging me." I didn't fall asleep easily; I didn't stay asleep well.

As I hadn't asked a question, Zane didn't answer. I waited quite a while before I realized he was gone.

The next day I ignored my food and water. I was hungry, I was thirsty, but I was scared too. I'd said I could hold out against seduction—if that's what this even was—and I could, but could I hold out against an eternity without my daughter? As the days became weeks, then years onto decades, and Jenna became older, then old, then ancient, and the time we had together was gone, what then?

The day after that Zane never showed up. Fine by me. I continued to ignore food and water, which made me so exhausted I nodded off in the afternoon when the lights of my prison were operating theater bright.

Gideon feathered his fingers across my face, then he kissed my cheek and tasted tears. "I'm sorry! I shouldn't have—"

"Oh, you definitely should have." Orgasms were awesome! "Can you do it again?"

His smile was slow, tentative, and full of wonder. "You know, no one's ever loved me."

"Not like I do." I brushed my hand up his back.

"No." Sadness flickered. "At all. No one's ever loved me at all."

"Those days are done," I promised. "I'll always love you. Always."

"I know," he whispered, then he touched me again the way that I wanted him to, the way I'd never known a girl could be touched, as if skin against skin were heart against heart.

A single brush of his thumb beneath the fullness of my breast, and I could not breathe. His lips at my earlobe, his tongue tracing my jaw, my collarbone, my rib, navel, and then the scent of walnuts washed over me.

Pulpy, syrupy, black as death, rotting-beneath-the-snow-and-the-leaves walnuts.

But that wasn't right. Gideon smelled of Ivory soap, a scent like gingerroot, clean and mellow and—

I tore myself out of the dream; the lights blared into my brain.

My head was resting on the table, inches away from the mashed potatoes I hadn't touched.

The rumble of Zane's voice, just out of sight and hushed. Made sense. Rotting walnuts equaled evil werewolf. And there he was.

My temple hurt a little. I must have smacked it into the unforgiving cherrywood. It would heal; I would heal. Forever and ever, into eternity, right here in this cave/prison if I couldn't—

Not now!

I made myself to breathe—in and out, a steady rhythm—and to remain exactly where I'd been, seemingly asleep. A voice I hadn't heard before—strangely soothing, appealingly deep—asked, "The plans?"

"Coming along splendidly." Zane sounded so pleased with himself I wanted to kick him. If I ever got near enough again, without a force field, I would.

"And the heir?"

My breath caught. Did this guy, whoever he was, know about Jenna? Did Zane?

But Jenna wasn't the heir because she wasn't a werewolf. I'd become one to keep her safe. I'd do it again, though, right now, being a werewolf wasn't helping me any.

"I've taken care of it."

What did that mean? Zane had taken care of Jenna becoming a werewolf or not becoming one? Was he even talking about her?

I'd killed Wendell before he could spill the beans—maybe. I wasn't sure when he'd discovered the beans, but even if he had shared them, why would he have shared them with Zane? They'd hated each other.

"Just make sure everyone who didn't agree to that damnable nose bump knows what's going on," Zane said.

While other packs fed on violence and chaos, Gideon's had control of their wolves because of him. There'd been some in Badru's pack who had not been on board with this, and as

Gideon had explained it, the wolf was always within, and unless we agreed to keep it there, even magic couldn't. Wolves that he had not made had to agree to his nose bump.

He'd believed they would come around eventually once they saw how much easier, how much safer and normal their lives would be if they did. But some people, some wolves, just liked to stir it up, and they weren't going to stop unless someone made them.

I swallowed the growl before it could erupt. The sound burned all the way to my stomach, where it bubbled in a cauldron of emptiness and acid.

I'd wondered before if Badru's wolves were now Zane's wolves, and it seemed like the holdouts were. A civil werewolf war approached, if we were lucky. If we weren't, the coup I'd suspected would become a slaughter.

"And you make sure you do what you promised," the unknown voice said.

"You doubt me?"

"If I didn't think you could deliver, I wouldn't be pledging my pack to your cause. I wouldn't be wasting my time to convince others."

Great. Zane had already gotten one pack, maybe more, to join his rebellion. Nothing worse than a psychopath with a cause. If he continued unchecked, shit was going to get real.

I had to *think*.

Gideon didn't trust Zane. Never had. Who would? He had to suspect this coup was coming. But he was distracted, searching for me. His beta should have been watching his flank. Instead, Gideon was also looking for a beta who was already, thanks to me, dead, burned to ashes, and fluttering on a distant breeze.

Because of what I'd done—I'd had no choice, Jenna's humanity had been at stake—Zane might succeed, and everything we'd done to stop the werewolf trafficking, the violence, and the murder and mayhem would start again. Unless I got out of here and warned Gideon, helped him, stood with him.

And the only way to do that was to give in.

But how to do so without tipping off Zane? I'd said I would never, that no matter what he did to me, I wouldn't agree to his terms of my release. And I'd meant it, so he would wonder *why now*? And I couldn't let him know I'd heard what he and the mystery asshole were saying.

I felt his gaze crawl up my back, then that rotting walnut scent hit me hard. Why hadn't I smelled it before when Zane was watching me? Magic something or other no doubt, definitely something that would make my head hurt and—

Problem at hand, Sarah! Problem at hand!

The scent drifted away, and I waited to the count of one hundred before I groaned, lifted my head, put my hands to my lower back, and rubbed. I got to my feet, turned, then gave a start that was not acting. Zane stood at the door, and I didn't smell anything but cave.

"What do you want?" I put just the right amount of *I'm exhausted, I'm hungry, thirsty, and I fell asleep with my head on the table long enough to make my back hurt, which I can't even shift to heal, thanks a lot, asshole* into my voice.

I'd been a senator's wife, fooled better than him.

Zane didn't answer because the answer was the same. What he wanted was me.

He spread his hands. They were nice hands, long fingers, wide palms. If he set one of those palms beneath my breast, if he cupped me, he could—

My nipples went so hard, I gasped. "Stop it."

He stood ten feet away, but I felt his thumb trace my stomach. I ground my teeth together to keep more than *stop it* from bursting free.

The air whispered my name; my hair fluttered against my temple.

"I can touch you here." Nipples again. "Or here." Stomach. "Perhaps both, if you would like." Palm to my belly, thumb to the right nipple, middle finger just a brush beneath the left. "I could take you from behind."

He still stood beyond the doorway, yet heat unfurled along my back.

"I could take you as a wolf."

"As wolves?" That could work.

"*Mais non.*" He chuckled, and the sound rumbled against my shoulders. "I could be a wolf, and you could be a woman."

Fur tickled my spine, though I still wore clothes, and he wasn't yet a wolf. I stiffened, and his lips seemed to brush my ear. "It is amazing. Let me show you."

"N-no."

"Fine." Disappointment laced his sigh. "As a man it is. But with my magic, I could take you one way and touch you another. My mouth could be on your neck and on your . . ." His lips curved, and his gaze dropped to my—

Clit, the air whispered.

Not a word I'd said or had said to me. Ever. Why did I like it? Because he was *making* me like it. Had to be.

"I could touch your breasts and make them . . ."

He waited, and while I knew what he was doing, I gave in anyway. "Make them what?"

He didn't answer, but my breasts swelled, they went tight and hot, and I bit my lip, hard, to keep in the moan.

"I could suckle you as I fuck you. You would not believe, Sarah, the things that I could do."

I already didn't.

"Is this what you're going to do?" I asked.

"This?" He stood before me, but his tongue brushed me in that place he'd named before, and I couldn't even nod. "*Oui.*"

"And then you'll let me out of here?" I waved at the cave walls, the force field-barred doorway.

"Oui."

"You promise not to tell Gideon?"

Zane laughed. "Of course, I'm going to tell him. Eventually."

There was the key to why. He didn't so much want the luna favor—sex with me—and deep down I'd known that; what he wanted was the consent so he could use it against Gideon, against me. For all I knew, cheating on the alpha was punishable by death. But as I'd already killed the beta, what was one more death sentence? They couldn't kill me twice.

Wait, maybe they could.

Oh well. This went beyond Gideon and me. I was the pack's luna, their mother, and just as I'd do anything for my daughter, I would do anything for them. Even die. Twice.

"All right."

Zane's eyes widened. Had I given in too easily? I didn't think so. Maybe I just needed to tell the truth. Or at least part of it. What lay at the heart of everything for me.

Jenna.

"I'm sick of this place, sick of you. I did all of this, I became this, for my daughter. I want to see her, so let's get 'er done."

"Get 'er done?" He seemed genuinely confused, but I didn't buy it.

"I have to say it out loud? Fine. Human sex, none of that wolf/woman kinky stuff."

His lips curved. "And the rest?"

"Yep. All of it. Works for me. Except this time finish. If I'm going to cheat"—even if it was to save a buttload of lives—"then I'm going to come."

The lights went out with a *thunk*.

"Pas de probleme," said the air that swirled around me. "Not a problem."

WHAT BETTER KNIFE THAN THIS?

I awoke in the light to someone calling my name.

Well, not *my* name—*Sarah*— but—

"Luna!"

I sat up, shoving the tangled hair from my face, snatching the quilt before it tumbled off my bare, still tingling from the orgasm of all orgasms, breasts, an instant before—

"Haley?"

—burst through the door.

Tall and slim, with silver-gold hair to her waist and gray-blue eyes, Haley resembled her uncle, the werewolf hunter, enough to make me misty.

"I need you to come with me, Your Maj—Luna."

I looked around. Yep, still in the dream Victorian bedroom recreated in a cave with glowing magic rock walls that had become my prison. "How are you here? *Are* you here?"

Fantasy and reality had gone wonky a while ago.

"Of course, I'm here." Haley picked up my discarded gold-flecked white robe, rolled her eyes, and tossed it aside before shrugging a backpack from her shoulders and pulling out a pair of sleep pants similar to the ones Zane had worn and a sweatshirt, which he hadn't, along with slip-on shoes. She handed the pile to me. "I figured you probably shifted at some point in the past several days."

"Thanks," I said, then I heard the rest of her sentence. "Wait. How long have I been gone?"

"Four days."

Haley suddenly seemed to see me—tousled, naked in a bed, my robe on the floor—and to put one and one together to make . . . one. "What did he do to you?"

Better question: What didn't he do?

Touches and tastes, a swirl of the wind, complete darkness enfolding me so that I could pretend he was—

Nope. Not going there.

"I'm fine." And I was. Very. "How did you find me?"

She reached for the quilt, and I growled. Didn't mean to, didn't even know I had until she snatched back her hand, then inched away, faced the wall. "It's my gift."

"Your . . ." I put my head through the neck of the sweatshirt. "What?"

"My magic."

"Right." Was my sluggish brain the result of the drugs I knew Zane had been giving me or from Zane himself? His body, my body, my sin, and my secret. For now.

I tried not to dwell on the idea that if I'd only held out one more day, I'd have been rescued before I'd granted him his luna favor.

Bad timing. Poor choices. A story as old as stories.

"What, exactly, *is* your magic?" As Zane had informed me shortly after I'd been changed, this question was considered rude in werewolf world. But I was the luna, so tough. Maybe because I was the luna, and she was my omega, Haley answered.

"I can find people, wolves. Well, both."

She would have been a handy minion to have back when Jenna had gone missing. Of course back then, in the golden days of yore—last week—I hadn't known about werewolves, or magic, or fucking magic werewolves. (Yeah, I heard that. Accidental double entendre.) And at that point, Haley hadn't yet been changed.

I finished tugging on the sleep pants. "I'm dressed."

She turned.

"How do you find people, wolves, wolf-people?"

Haley ducked her head. "I . . . um . . . taste their blood."

"Say what?"

She flinched. I had said that pretty loud, but from the echoing silence in the caves, and Haley's unchallenged entrance, Zane was gone. And he'd taken his force field with him.

He had agreed to release me if I granted him my favor. Still, I'd expected him to pull something shady, at the least make me remind him, perhaps make me beg. That he'd just disappeared and left the gate hanging open . . . I didn't trust it, and I was sure it was only a matter of time until I ran face-first into whatever booby trap he'd fashioned just for me.

I laid my hand on Haley's arm and kept it there until she lifted her gaze. "Sorry. I'm still getting used to all this."

Haley should be, too, but she seemed to be adapting well. Which made me feel like a loser until I remembered she was twenty years younger. Easier to change your life—your species—without all the baggage.

"Go on," I urged.

Her brow creased. "I . . . um . . . that's it."

"You can't drop that one and not elaborate." I splayed my fingers and swept my hand, indicating we should exit my boudoir. Immediately. "You taste someone's blood, and you . . .?"

"See where they are." She preceded me into the empty corridor. "Which is why it took me a while to find you."

"Force field," I muttered.

She frowned.

"Zane can do spells."

She nodded. Apparently, I was the only one that had been news to.

"He shazammed a shimmery door thing right . . ." I pointed at the archway we'd just stepped through. "Today, not so much."

"That makes sense. This morning everything cleared, and I saw you."

I was just glad she hadn't seen me last night. If she had, she wouldn't have been asking what Zane had done. She would know. Small favors.

"There aren't a lot of caves in Wisconsin," I said, "but there are more than one."

Haley shook her head. "I don't—"

"You figured out what cave I was in by seeing it? Are you a spelunker?"

I didn't know what she'd done before she'd done this—omega to my luna—something no little girl would aspire to, though exploring and studying caves probably wasn't on that list either.

"A what? Oh!" Understanding dawned. "No. Once I see"—she shrugged—"I go there."

"But how do you know where to go?"

"I just go." She flipped the fingers of both hands into the air.

"Oh!" Understanding dawned on me too. "Magic. Right!" Still not bridging that gap to magic without a lot of explanation. I decided to blame menopause brain. Had to be good for something. "But why would you taste anyone's blood?"

"Ma'am?"

"I mean, I wouldn't." *Uck*. "You thought it would be a good idea to put blood in your mouth and voilà? Magic?"

"It was more of a compulsion. An urging toward the gift. Didn't you feel it when you discovered your own?"

My own was making people believe my lies. Had I been

compelled to lie? That was a tough one. Weren't we all compelled to lie when lying was necessary?

"Where did you get my blood?"

"The window."

Getting info out of this kid was almost as hard as getting it out of Zane.

I thought back. The last window I'd touched had been . . . "At Jenna's?"

There had been a lot of blood. I'd been drenched in it, but I'd showered, and the blood had not been mine.

"When you went out, you scratched your leg, your arm . . . something."

I had been on the run, too busy to worry about a scratch, even if I'd noticed it, and any injury would have healed the first time I changed.

"And you were there why?"

"I was ordered to find you, protect you. And I couldn't. I didn't."

"That wasn't your fault."

"Tell it to Alpha."

"Oh, I will."

Her lips curved. "I thought about where you might be, and the obvious answer was your daughter's."

Except Jenna wouldn't have told Haley that I'd been there any more than she'd told Gideon.

"What did she—?"

"I never talked to her. I saw the open window, went to check, saw the blood, and then—" She spread her hands.

She'd tasted it. E*w*. "And then?"

"I saw you knocking on the door of a log home."

Explained how Gideon had found out where I was. No idea how Zane had, and what did it matter now?

"Then things went hazy and poofed out altogether."

I smiled at *poofed out*, though that's probably what had

happened once Zane and his magic spells showed up. But today, when the spell was lifted because I'd—

Nope. Putting that in the rearview, along with the specifics of Haley's "gift." Had she had to taste my blood again to get here, and if so, how had she? Could a scratch have produced enough blood to keep extra, perhaps dried in a plastic bag?

Why did my brain go to these places?

"Well, thanks."

Haley inclined her head. "We need to hurry."

I figured she meant, *get gone before the psycho, evil werewolf I'd fucked for my freedom, and hadn't needed to, came back from wherever he'd gone and decided, despite his promise—because that's what psycho, evil werewolves did—to kidnap me again and Haley, too, just for kicks.*

I started for the entrance.

Haley snatched my arm. "No time." Then she popped her index finger into her mouth, and right before everything went swirly, I saw that finger was the shade of dried serial murder.

Then I couldn't breathe, couldn't see, couldn't move or escape. Ever wonder what being caught in a tornado is like? Don't. It hurt. Everywhere. And my ears!

Wha-wha-wha. A maddening pulse and release of sound that made my head feel as if it might burst outward like a pumpkin when it hit the asphalt.

Then everything stopped so suddenly I still heard the *whaaaa,* still felt the wind, and my head felt the whirl. I opened my eyes, but they were watering so badly I couldn't see. If Haley hadn't been holding my elbow, I'd have fallen. Then my ears cleared, my eyes too, and I looked up, up, up, turned my head left, then right.

"Why the hell are we at Camp Randall?"

I hadn't gone to college, but I had gone to a butt-ton of football games, always during an election year. Alumni loved to vote for one of their own, and Patrick made a point of advertising his political science cum law degree from the University of Wisconsin, as well as his daughter's attending his alma mater.

The best way to get the most mileage? By dressing up in red and white from head to toe, then attending a football game at the oldest stadium in the Big Ten, capacity over 80,000 "jumping around" fans, have them announce your name, wave at the jumbotron, and smile, smile, smile.

From the length of the lines waiting to get in, whatever was happening wasn't a sellout, but the seats were going to be pretty full.

"You need to stop the blood-sport battle," Haley said.

"The what now?"

She snatched my hand and towed me along. I probably shouldn't allow it, I was the luna after all, but the kid had saved me—well, she'd meant to, how could she know I'd already saved myself?—and she seemed pretty upset.

"It's what the patricians—the rich people, the ones in the front row—called the gladiator fights in the Roman Colosseum."

More oval than round but built with an open roof and a lotta stone, Camp Randall looked a lot like the Colosseum. Named for Alexander Randall, who'd been governor at the beginning of the Civil War, the grounds had once been a training area and staging point for Union recruits, later a Confederate prison camp; both the state fair and Barnum Circus, before it had merged with Bailey, had called this stretch of ground their home. Now, the Badgers did.

I knew such minutia because, as a senator's wife, I'd learned that historical trivia made a better sound bite than "Great game!" and in Wisconsin, one did not ask, "What's a first down?"

"And why are we using this term in the twenty-first century?" I asked.

Haley led me toward a less-crowded gate. "Lucius Falto was a patrician. Now he's in charge of—" She flipped a hand upward as we entered the building.

"A werewolf from ancient Rome is in charge of Camp Randall?"

"Yes. Which makes it simple for him to organize any blood sports, basically executions couched in entertainment. For werewolves."

I took a moment to absorb that. I could see the appeal. If anyone in my family was murdered, I'd love to toss the guilty into a ring with a werewolf or ten and then watch, wouldn't you?

"These are all werewolves?"

"When the moon comes up."

Werewolves. Moon. Right.

"Why here? Why . . . this?"

"A blood-sport execution is a big deal. Considering the logistics, permission isn't granted very often, and it's only granted in serious cases. Because of the rarity, thousands have come to watch. Tens of thousands maybe by the time the moon lifts into the sky."

Gideon controlled two packs. How many wolves to a pack? I wasn't sure. Not more than a few hundred. Maybe. He wasn't the only alpha, but—

"Tens of . . . *thousands*? Of *werewolves*?"

She glanced uneasily at the crowd streaming past us and toward their seats, then lowered her voice. "My family has killed a lot of them for a long, long time. My uncle is going to pay the price for that."

"Ash believed he was killing mass murderers in a wolf coat. Considering Zane, a lot of the time he probably was."

"Except he didn't kill Zane, and that was a mistake because werewolves have family too."

"Zane doesn't. He's a lone wolf, a sigma, not the same as the rest."

I still couldn't figure out why Badru had not only accepted Zane but made him his beta. And considering Badru was ashes to ashes, just like Wendell, I wouldn't find out. Zane wasn't telling.

"Once Badru accepted him instead of killing him, Zane wasn't a lone wolf anymore."

"Badru's pack was his pack."

"At least until Alpha took them."

He hadn't taken all of them. Did Gideon know that?

"Where is he?"

"Alpha will be in the premium seating."

Of course, he would. I'd sat in several of the suites during my Mrs. Senator Sullivan days. They were luxurious, but right now, they were giving me Abe Lincoln vibes.

"Is every werewolf in the US coming to this thing?"

"All are welcome."

"How did they find out about it?"

"Private Facebook group. Phone chain. Group texts."

I stifled a burst of laughter at the thought of a werewolf group text.

"Only those who've lost a loved one because of my family," Haley continued, "can put their name into the lottery—more than one loss, more than one ticket."

"And what do they win, Regis?"

Her lips twitched. She'd gotten one of my pop culture references. If I'd had time to be excited, I would have been.

"They win a place in line to the killing floor."

"Ash is going to have to fight his way out of here through werewolves?"

"It's an execution, Luna. There is no way out. They're going to throw werewolves at him until one of them wins."

"But Gideon vowed to let *Zane* deal with the hunter."

"Zane was given the choice of what to do with my uncle, and he chose this."

"He doesn't want to hold the knife himself, twist it a bit?"

I didn't realize Haley had led me up a ramp until we could see the stadium lifting all around us. She indicated the rows and rows of concrete steps and the steadily filling section upon section of bench seating, not to mention those patrician luxury suites.

"What better way? What better knife than this?"

She had a point.

"It's going to be a spectacle," Haley said, despair weighting her voice, her face, her very being.

"Like hell it is."

SHIT, SHIT, SHIT ABOUT COVERED IT

"Where's your uncle?"

Ash had found my daughter. Kind of. Jenna hadn't really been lost, but neither one of us had known that. He'd walked into the wolf's den with me, been captured because of me. I couldn't just leave him here.

Haley's smile blossomed. "I knew you'd help."

"You didn't give me much choice."

Confusion flickered. "You're the luna. You have all the choices."

I supposed I'd had the choice between letting Jenna become a werewolf and volunteering for it myself. Or I could have let Wendell change her, negating my first not-really-a-choice, instead of killing him. But when compared to what had happened to Haley—family murdered, kidnapped as bait, turned against her will—she had a point.

"Let's get him out of here."

Haley led me away from the milling crowd. "They're keeping him in the McClain Center somewhere." At my frown, she continued. "Locker rooms, offices, cafeteria, and so on. Shouldn't be too hard to find him."

"There are gonna be minions."

There always were. But considering everyone else would be streaming into the stadium proper for the coming extravaganza taking place in the arena/football field, those minions were going to be a flashing neon arrow pointing straight to our destination.

"But you can push people."

I frowned. "How do you know that?"

"I'm your omega. I need to know these things, so Alpha told me."

Her expression—hurt and disappointment—revealed Gideon had also shared how I'd pushed her.

"I'm sorry, I—"

She shook her head, shrugged. "It'll be helpful today."

"It will." Though I had to wonder why since Zane knew I had this power, he had let me out.

Because he'd figured I would flounder around in the cave and/or the forest for a while—at least until the moon rose. By then it would be too late for me to do anything even if, for some unknown reason, it occurred to me that every werewolf in the Midwest and beyond was at Camp Randall for an execution.

"That'll get him out of his cage and away from the minions, but getting him out of here . . ." I threw up both hands. "I'm not sure if I can push tens of thousands to believe what I say." And if I couldn't, we were screwed.

Haley bit her lip. My brain sped one way, then another, then rolled around and around a while before I concluded . . . "Making a run for it is all I got, and I don't think that's gonna work."

Haley held up one finger. "If we had a place to hide him, I could get some blood and transport him out."

"Get some blood?"

"It's easy enough."

I let that pass. Maybe I was getting the hang of this luna job. Or failing at it miserably.

"Even if you managed to get him out, he might stab you in the back the first chance he gets."

Ash was very single-minded. He believed that a werewolf was a werewolf was a werewolf. No exceptions. He had reasons, most of them pretty good ones.

Ash would as soon blast Haley with a silver bullet as look at her, no matter who she was, or rather who she'd been. He'd tried once, shot me by accident instead, but bygones and all that.

Haley turned her head, lifted a staying hand, then crooked her fingers once in a *follow me* gesture. She stopped at the end of hall, peeked around the corner, and her shoulders sank. When I caught up, I saw why.

Two man-wolves I'd met before—Dirty Blond and Triangle Head—marched out of a door beyond which a shiny team locker room lived. Red and white *W*s abounded, cushy recliners, brand-new carpet in a hue I didn't even try to name—I hadn't thought something could be bland if it contained so many colors. But I'd been wrong.

I stepped forward, orders to stand by the wall, stare at the ceiling, and forget I'd ever come near them on the tip of my tongue, but Haley threw out an arm, shook her head.

Two more hulks dragged Ash between them through the door; another duo followed. The latter duo I'd also seen before; one of them had fought in the Crusades. That he was still a follower, not a leader, made me wonder how many times he'd been clobbered on that huge head by an even huger sword, similar to the one both he and his buddy carried now.

The blade sparked silver beneath the fluorescent lights, the hilt obviously not silver or it would have fried off his hand. They must expect werewolf trouble—perhaps someone who had drawn a number in the thousands from the "Slaughter-Ash" lottery and wasn't in the mood to wait.

"They won't kill him," Haley whispered. "But they can cut him, hurt him, make him b-b-bleed."

And from the looks of him, Ash couldn't afford to be cut, hurt, or made to bleed any more than he already had been. Not if we wanted him to keep breathing long enough to get him out of here.

The grape-pulp black eyes he'd had when I'd last seen him had lightened in places to a Wicked Witch green, in others to a lovely bile yellow. The blood in his hair resembled the rusted undercarriage of a '57 Desoto rather than crimson head injury. He'd managed to wrap one hand with strips from his torn and blood-stained shirt, but he listed to the side, favoring no doubt cracked ribs. He wasn't going to last through one werewolf, let alone however many there were in the lottery line.

Haley and I slipped from one corner to another, to a doorway, behind a sports drink machine, anywhere we could find so we could keep Ash in sight and us out of it.

The cadre trooped beneath a sign—*The Road to the Rose Bowl Begins Here,* complete with a rose—up a tunnel painted French vanilla. They paused at the apex, silhouetted in a rectangle of approaching twilight, and twelve pairs of minion eyes became glued to the field.

I didn't think; I ran.

"Luna!" Haley said, and she didn't whisper.

Luckily, or unluckily as it turned out, a booming voice filled the stadium at the same time. "Welcome one and all!"

I reached the middle of the ramp and touched my forehead. "Backs against—"

The sound system blared, "And now for the main event!" followed by the *bum-bum-bump, bum-bum-bump* rhythm of stomps and claps to the beat of *We Will Rock You* from the rest of the stadium, which drowned out the remainder of my order.

However, those two words were enough to draw the attention of the seven men before me.

Ash's eyes opened as wide as they were able, and his lips formed the word *Sarah*!

Five of the hulks stared at me stupidly, but one had a brain. He shoved Ash toward the field. He seemed to have a lot more strength than he should have, even for someone his size, because Ash flew off his feet and landed out of sight.

The nearest one reached for me, and I smacked my palm against my forehead harder than I needed to, but I was pissed. I'd been so close. "All six wolves go to the parking lot and beat the crap out of one another for a few hours."

Their black eyes and broken bones would heal as soon as they shifted, but they'd hurt. And right now I wanted them to.

They marched past me single file. Good riddance.

I crept forward as close as I could get so that I could see but, I hoped, not be seen by anyone who might care.

The *bum-bum-bump* slowly faded to silence.

"Now on the field we have the hunter."

"Boooooo!" rose from the crowd as Ash slowly, painfully got to his feet.

"Shit, shit, shit!" Haley joined me.

I said nothing as *shit, shit, shit* about covered it.

"And the number one selection in our lottery, Otto Schmidt."

On the other side of the field, Otto, a stout little man with thinning gray hair, lifted his arms to the sky, and the crowd cheered.

In a normal world, Otto would get his ass kicked. But the world wasn't normal. It never had been.

"*Gauleiter* Schmidt will be fighting to avenge the death of his son, *Hauptsturmführer* Schmidt of the *Schutzstaffel*."

"What the hell did he just say?"

"*Gauleiter* is the third highest rank in the Nazi Party; *Hauptsturmführer* is equivalent to the rank of captain." Haley's gaze flicked to me, then back to her uncle. "In the SS."

I knew there were Nazis. There shouldn't be, but there were. However, the SS . . . hadn't that lovely collection of assholes gone the way of Hitler?

The unseen announcer continued. "*Hauptsturmführer* Schmidt died protecting the castle where Herr Mengele created the *Führer's* werewolf army."

I turned to Haley and spread my hands in a "what the fucking fuck?" gesture.

"Long story," Haley said. "Not now."

"According to our *Book of Books,* magic is not allowed in this ring any more than it's allowed in the ring of challenge."

"Because bein' a werewolf ain't magic," I muttered.

"The field has been blessed by the Hakim," Haley said.

Blessed was a strange thing to call the shimmering circle of fog I'd once seen the werewolves own personal sorcerer trail from his fingertips. But it prevented a werewolf from using magic, as well as leaving the ring unless he or she wanted to be zapped with an electric charge so hot it lit your fur on fire.

I didn't see that filmy circle now, but who knew where the Hakim—a man of indeterminate age and incredible height who resembled a praying mantis, all legs and elbows and buggy eyes—had placed it.

"The Hakim also warded the stadium. From outside, humans see only the usual dark, empty building in the middle of the night. They won't hear anything either."

I had wondered what the neighbors were going to think of a gazillion people streaming into the stadium after midnight. Now I knew. They wouldn't think anything because they wouldn't see anything.

Sorcerers were damned handy to have on the payroll.

"And if someone wanders in?"

Haley cast me a glance. "Let's hope they don't."

In other words, they wouldn't be getting back out.

"Otto has been waiting decades for his vengeance." The announcer's voice drew our attention back to the field. "And now his time has come. Do you have anything to say for yourself, hunter?"

It occurred to me even before Ash shrugged, barely managing to hide the wince from the pain his nonchalant movement caused his ribs, and said, "Wasn't me"—mysteriously amplified though no physical means I could see—that he couldn't have been running around Nazi Germany blasting werewolves. He hadn't even been born.

"Obviously," murmured a voice I'd heard once before. "It was me."

"Grandfather," Haley whispered.

Awesome. The greatest werewolf hunter of all time had arrived.

A BIGGER, BETTER MONSTER

I'd glimpsed the old man during a FaceTime call with Ash. In person, Edward looked slightly less "ancient-should-be-dead" than he had on the iPhone. Perhaps because, in person, he moved like a much, *much* younger man than he could possibly be.

Tall and gaunt, he still had most of his hair, even though it had faded to a golden-tinged silvery white that reminded me of his grandson's before it had taken a rust-tinted bath.

Edward's piercing gaze, the shade of January ice, went to Haley, and I stepped in front of her.

His thin lips curved. "If I were here for her, you would not be able to stop me."

He obviously didn't know what I was, and I should probably keep it that way as long as I could, considering. But if he didn't know about me, how did he know about her?

"*Liebchen,* do not tease."

The beauty of the woman who emerged from the smoky shadows of the corridor and laid a graceful hand on the shoulder of the hunter sparkled as brightly as her still-vivid deep-blue eyes. Her hair had gone nearly white, though here and there amid the close-cropped curls a strand of obsidian remained.

"*La Mémé*." Haley's voice brimmed with love.

Her great-grandmother. The voodoo queen.

The woman contemplated Haley with true fondness. "Ignore him, *engel*."

Hearing German pronounced with an upper-class French accent made an already surreal situation even more so.

"I . . . I don't think I can," Haley said.

"Or probably should." I kept my gaze on the old man, alert for any fast moves, though from what I could tell, he wasn't packing beneath the knee-length black leather coat. "Why *are* you here?"

"Haley called her grandmother, confessed what she had become, then begged us to save her uncle."

I indicated the Colosseum. "Good luck with that."

"Why are *you* here?" he asked.

"To get Ash out."

The old man's desperately-in-need-of-a-trim parchment-white eyebrows lifted. "Common ground. How lovely."

Nothing about this was lovely.

"Ash spoke to me of you," Edward said. "Of how devoted you were to finding your child, how brave. I appreciate your wanting to help him, but we are here now."

"Doesn't everyone in this place know who you are?" He'd been around long enough.

"They might know who I am, but they don't know what I look like."

"How'd you manage that?"

"Because every werewolf that's ever seen him is dead," Haley said.

"Eh." Edward waggled his hand.

Haley continued to hover behind me, and it made me feel warm and gooey inside—the way I'd felt when Jenna had snuggled into me whenever she was afraid as a child—that Haley trusted me to protect her, even as the considering expression in *La Mémé's* stormy eyes gave me a chill. I knew what she was thinking. Why would Haley hide behind me if she was already, according to the old man's theories, a monster?

Because I was the bigger, better monster.

I waited for the call-out, but *La Mémé* said nothing.

A cheer went up from the spectators. The sound became louder and louder, lengthening into a howl from the throats of thousands as the moon crested the horizon and silver spilled across the sky.

My head buzzed; I couldn't think. The moon called.

Haley's lips brushed my ear. "She isn't full. We can resist if we stay out of the direct moonlight."

The lopsided orb was hard to ignore, but considering this badass werewolf hunter and his werewolf hunting, voodoo queen wife didn't know what I was, I needed to. Here and there, around the stadium, others hadn't changed either—those who probably needed opposable thumbs for one reason or another. At least it made Edward and *La Mémé* less conspicuous.

In the ring, they handed Ash a stick. A big stick, but still. A stick! To fight a werewolf.

"We have to help him," Haley said.

"Wait." The old man lifted a finger. "Every hunter holds back a secret, last chance."

"What—?"

He stepped closer, and I managed, barely, not to step back. "Let Ash have his fun while I tell you my plan."

I glanced at his wife, who turned graceful hands palms up. "My love is still breathing because he knows what he is doing, *mezanmi*."

She was the reason they were both breathing, and while I thought it hypocritical to use magic to stay so perky in order to kill magic werewolves, I should probably keep that to myself.

Otto had shifted quick as spit into a roly-poly, steel-wool-gray wolf, the speed of his change a mark of the old as hell.

At least Otto wouldn't bite Ash because having his quarry turn into a werewolf, making this an actual fair fight, was not what any of them wanted. Instead, the ancient Nazi stalked forward, herding Ash toward the center of the fifty-yard line, which was no doubt the best place to tear out his throat so that everyone could see.

"Your attention, *ja?*"

Edward opened his black leather coat like a fifties cartoon flasher. Thank God he wasn't naked. No one, save *La Mémé* perhaps, wanted to see that. Beneath it he had explosives strapped here, hanging there.

I hadn't thought he was packing, but I'd been wrong.

"Holy hell!" I tugged the coat closed. "Are you on crack?"

"Not since nineteen forty . . ." He looked up, considering, then at his wife. "*Mezanmi?*"

His French was also excellent and also off because of his accent, but his use of the same word for her as she'd used for me made me think it did not mean *bitch*. Good to know.

"Forty-three, I believe."

I stepped back and glanced over my shoulder at Haley, eyebrows raised, before just as quickly returning my attention to Edward. Best not to take my eyes off him for too long.

Haley shrugged so close to me I felt the up, then down heat of it along my back. "He was a spy during World War Two. A *kriminalrat,* a major. Gestapo."

Renée made *pshaw* sound. "He was not Gestapo. He only pretended."

"Double agent," I said. "I bet you were pretty good at it."

"I had to be."

"So the rumors of the Reich being amped on coke are true?"

"Not coke so much as crystal meth, but—"

"Whatever!" I waved my hand at his explosive cache. "I can't let you hurt all these pe—"

"Let?" The old man chuckled, and his gaze flicked to his wife. "She's adorable."

"Edward . . ." Renée's tone held a warning, which he ignored.

"They are not people."

Edward sounded so much like a grumpy old man—he was a grumpy old man—I wanted to laugh, but considering the sitch, I just couldn't.

I'd had this argument with Ash, gotten the same headache. Nevertheless, I drew breath to . . . I'm not sure what. Argue more with someone you couldn't argue with? Scream for help from . . . no idea. The only people in this arena who'd ever helped me were the man in the ring with a werewolf and a stick, the no-longer-only-a-man in the premium suite watching it, and the no-longer-only-a-girl hiding behind me, none of whom were going to.

The sound I made—a combo of disgust, confusion, and fury—made Edward's indulgent smile return. "Calm yourself."

My eyes narrowed. What was the saying?

Telling a woman to calm herself worked as well as baptizing a cat.

"Even if I brought down the house, so to speak, they wouldn't die." He lifted withered, veined hands like a revivalist preacher. "This isn't a solid silver building, and so far, we haven't been able to invent silver dynamite."

"But we're still trying," Renée said.

I couldn't tell if she was kidding or not.

"Though what we have invented works very, very well when placed correctly," Edward said.

I wanted to ask about the inventions, hell, I wanted to ask about a lot of things, but another glance into the ring revealed it was time for me to fly.

I shoved Haley in the direction of *La Mémé*. "Keep her safe."

As I ran across the fifty-yard line, I wished I could do so faster and more gracefully than the forty-one-year-old woman I was.

Luckily no one was watching me; they had all gone eerily silent, intent on the display of Otto with his fangs poised over Ash's throat.

"Stop!" My shout cut the expectant silence like a newly sharpened knife through crisp, white paper.

After a collective canine *pfff*, thousands of wolf eyes lifted to Gideon, standing in one of those luxury suites, still human, no doubt so he could give the thumbs-up or a thumbs-down like . . . like . . . I don't know . . . Caligula?

A quick glance revealed that the *Jager-Sucher* lord and lady had gone, I hoped to blow shit up and not stab their great-granddaughter with a silver dagger. I shoved that image right out of my head.

Thousands of throats howled, "Boooooooooo!" and I spun.

Every hunter holds back a secret, last chance.

A circle of flame sprang up from Otto's steel-wool fur and the scent of burned hair mixed with that of blood an instant before Ash, somehow on his knees and not his back, twisted the silver wire he'd wrapped around the old Nazi's throat; the wolf's head imploded.

Nasty wolf innards sprayed all over Ash. I wasn't close enough to get more than a spatter. Last week that would have made me shriek and run for the hills, if not a shower. Today it barely slowed me down.

I caught Ash as he toppled over. "Hey. *Hey*! Stay with me."

He nodded, but his eyes were closed, and there was so much blood, and other things, on him I couldn't get a good grip; he took us both to the ground.

Heat blistered my left side. Otto had gone up in flames. Silver had that effect on werewolves. I was surprised he had imploded, *then* caught fire. Hadn't seen that before. As he burned, he twisted and turned and morphed into a man. That I had seen.

A gash in Ash's forearm trickled fresh streaks the shade of coup de gras, and I slapped my hand over it, then pressed. The wound wasn't a bite, not jagged and toothy enough, but it could be from a claw.

"Wire," Ash mumbled.

"It's right here." I nearly pulled it close, then remembered. Silver. No touchies. "Where'd you get it?"

He flexed his hand, and the slice in his skin wept blood against my own.

It took me a minute to connect things. "You had a silver wire in your arm." Explained the gash. "Your secret last chance."

His eyes opened. "The only ones who know that are—"

Before he could say the words that any old werewolf might hear, considering the magically amped sound system, and blow things sky high before things blew sky high, I did the only thing I could.

I kissed him.

INCREDIBLY INAPPORPRIATE FOR AN EXECUTION

The gasp from the crowd wasn't so much a gasp as the sound a British matron would make following a social gaffe instead of a combined huff from a thousand-plus werewolf snouts.

I tasted blood—how could I not?—and my wolf fairly purred. I couldn't resist licking his lips, and when he licked mine back—oh my!

Down, girl!

Ash peered into my face. His brow creased.

Dammit! My eyes had probably gone aquamarine—the jeweled tones of my wolf crowding out the more easily explainable but definitely prettier than they had been cerulean of every day.

I lowered my gaze and whispered, "Be ready."

He nodded, then heaved me away. I was so shocked I hit the gadrillion-dollar FieldTurf like a bag of beans. They could say it was like landing on clouds, but it wasn't.

By the time I got my breath back, minions had taken away the silver wire—using gloves, pussies—then glided what must have been a metal detector over Ash as he struggled and cursed and bled.

One of them waved a meaty arm in a clockwise circular motion, something I'd seen from referees during the multiple football games I'd endured. My brain translated: *No timeouts. Ball in play. Clock is running.* In other words: *Next!*

What was taking Edward so long?

The PA announcer, who must have been waiting for the signal, used his *Are you ready to rumble?* voice, which I found incredibly inappropriate for an execution.

"And now for our second-place winner! You are gonna love this one, folks! Originally from Judea . . ."

Yipping and howling commenced. They knew the entrant from Judea. From the way Ash went pale beneath the blood, he did too.

"Now residing in Las Vegas, that City of Sin!"

"Who is it?"

As if in answer, the Michael Buffer wannabe—that could not actually be Michael Buffer, could it?—continued. "Humans know him as Jude Sicariot!"

"The rock star?" My voice rose to new heights. "He's a werewolf?"

"That ain't all," Ash said.

"But we know him as Judas. That's right, folks, Judas Iscariot."

"I thought he hung himself."

"As he didn't do so with a silver rope," Ash murmured, "didn't take."

"Jude's entry into the lottery was the killing of one of his many, many wives."

"Wasn't just one."

The nose of the minion who held Ash on the right flared wide like a bull's; the fingernails of the one who held him on the left popped into claws, drawing speckles of blood from Ash's arm. I should probably put a stop to that, but I was still reeling with the revelation that Judas—*the* Judas—was Jude Sicariot, one of the biggest rock stars in the history of rock.

And a werewolf.

From the tunnel where the home team emerged on game day erupted a sound more like the roar of an erupting volcano than the snarl of the hulking, gargantuan wolf-shaped shadow, which lurched closer and closer and—

Judas/Jude emerged from the tunnel, and the crowd went wild.

The creature had long ebony hair that undulated along a muscular body, catching the moonlight and flashing neon blue across the non-grass. The ebony eyes would have blended in if they hadn't sparkled like the surface of Lunar Lake in the depths of the night.

"How?" I whispered. "Why is he so big?"

The human Jude was heroin skinny and maybe three inches taller than me, which brought him in at five-seven-ish. Now that I knew he hailed from the land of late BC, maybe early AD, that made sense. He'd probably been considered tall back then.

This wolf was the largest I'd ever seen, not that I'd seen many. From claws to shoulder, he had to be over six feet, add his head to that, and if he lifted onto his hind legs . . . I couldn't even do that math.

"He's a Lycanon. Greek," Left Minion said. "The older they get, the bigger they become, the stronger, the meaner, the harder to kill. This is gonna be awesome."

"As you all know," the announcer continued, voice far too jolly, "Judas's punishment for his transgression was lycanthropy."

"Thirty pieces of silver."

I hadn't realized I'd said that out loud until Right Minion answered, "He could never touch them."

Had that been the original, "let the punishment fit the crime"? If so, bravo.

"Is that why silver kills you?"

Kills us.

Right Minion shrugged. "Maybe."

He lifted his gaze to the alpha. Gideon didn't even look at me, just flicked a hand toward the exit, and both minions dropped Ash like a leper, then headed for me.

I would have been irritated by the flippant behavior, but the sight of Zane sleazily slinking along the corridor in Gideon's direction, wolf shadows skulking at his side, made concern overcome my annoyance.

"Wait!"

The minions did not wait; they lifted me off my feet and began to cart me away.

I struggled, but it was like fighting quicksand when you were holding an anvil. "There's going to be a coup."

Had this entire show been part of Zane's plot? In ridding himself, ridding all the werewolves, of Ash, he would have his revenge, but in drawing everyone's attention *to* that revenge, he would create the perfect situation to take out Gideon.

"Zane is up there with Badru's wolves, the ones that are his now, and probably some others he's recruited. They're going to—You need to—"

The minions kept marching.

What to do, what to do? The enormous werewolf lurched closer to Ash. The other monster closed in on Gideon. Could I save them both? I had to try. But first monster first . . .

The minions either weren't smart, or they weren't thinking—maybe both, the two did go hand in hand—or perhaps they thought the Hakim's charmed circle would keep me from shifting. I wasn't certain about that either. Maybe they just didn't see the thin shaft of silver peeking over the scoreboard and trickling across the fake grass. They walked too close, and I trailed a foot through it, hoping that, with my mind too scattered to focus on the shift, this would be enough to give me a boost.

The moon launched both chill and heat into the soul Ash

would soon no longer think I had; I reached for my wolf, and I changed.

Suddenly all paws and claws, fur and teeth, the minions bobbled me, and I was gone across the FieldTurf, flipping bits of sand and rubber and poly-something-or-other fibers behind me as I dug in and leaped, putting myself between Ash and the were wolf rock star.

The monstrous beast lifted his snout to the moon and howled. I took the offensive and yanked out a chunk of his massive chest. The howl curled into a snarl, and he lifted a gargantuan paw; the stadium lights glinted off claws as long and sharp as medieval swords an instant before he—

Kaboom!

The force of the explosion tossed me sideways. Even better, a crevasse opened, and Judas's front paws slid in. He became occupied saving his own ass, and he wasn't paying attention to mine.

Ash skittered away from me, almost fell into another hole. Above Gideon's suite, the overhang crumbled. In the corridor, concrete fell—sharp thuds followed by crunches as some hit the seats, then yelps and whimpers as some hit wolves. Zane and his coup-posse disappeared in a cloud of rock and dust.

We should probably get while the gettin' was still possible.

I ran a few steps, looked back. Ash stared at me without comprehension. Lassie I wasn't. Or maybe he was just in shock. You'd think a werewolf hunter would be less inclined, but he'd had a few surprises, on top of the head injuries.

I could change, grab his hand, pull him along, try to explain, but I'd be naked. Not that it mattered in the scheme of things, but considering the audience, I should probably keep my claws and teeth a while longer. Once I herded him out of here, I'd circle back for Gideon.

The lights went out with a *thunk*. We didn't really need them, we had the moon, but their sudden loss felt ominous.

"When, Sarah? Why?"

Ash knew why. Jenna. I hadn't told him she was Gideon's child, though he probably suspected. When? That he didn't know, and I was in no position to tell him that the second time he'd kissed me I'd already been this.

Judas yanked one paw out of the crevasse, and with shining dark eyes amplified by fury, he zeroed in on Ash, then began to gnaw on the other one. From the size of his jaws, that wasn't gonna take long.

I lifted my snout in that direction, and once Ash looked, he had no problem putting aside questions of why and when, at least for the time being, in order to hoof it for the exit. Silhouetted in the moonlight now spilling through the archway, a too tall, obscenely thin man slunk away.

The Hakim was gettin' while the getting' was still possible as well.

With all the rubble, it took longer than I wanted it to for us to reach that archway, and before we could go through it, Gideon stepped in our way.

Relief flooded me. He was safe.

A sudden rat-a-tat of gunfire erupted. That was a lot of bullets for the police, and who were they shooting at anyway? Then I saw Ash's smirk. Not the police but more *Jager-Suchers,* and my recent decision to keep my claws and teeth a tad longer went out the window.

I had to warn Gideon, so I reached for my inner Sarah, and the instant I could form words, I blurted, "Edward's here."

"Mandenauer?"

I'd never heard the old man's last name. "*Jager-Sucher* dude?"

Gideon gave a sharp nod.

"Then, yes. You need to go."

"After this little stunt"—Gideon flicked a dismissive hand at Ash—"so do you. What were you thinking?"

I'd been thinking I wasn't going to let the man who'd come

when I needed him, who'd risked his life more than once to help me, die if I could save him. Gideon knew that, therefore the question was rhetorical, and I ignored it.

Ash's gaze shifted to the sea of dust-covered, naked once-wolves and furry still-wolves that burst out of every exit and loped down the streets. I took an instant to be glad he had no more weapons. In the distance, sirens wailed.

I stepped in close to Gideon, and my bare breasts brushed his one-size-too-small mustard-gold T-shirt. I kissed him quick, before he could stop me. "Thank you for loving me, for *choosing* me, even though—" My voice broke. "Even though you knew that taking me as your mate would be the end of everything you've come to hold dear."

"This sounds like good-bye."

It was, but I couldn't let him know that, or he'd never leave. Considering the shouts, the gunfire, the scent of burned—nope, not thinking about what was burning—he needed to.

A posse of his wolves congregated behind him. The way they bristled, the way they stared—glared—they weren't going to leave without him. Or me. Unless I lied and well. This was becoming my specialty.

"I'll get Haley, then we'll meet at our house." I was going to miss that house and everything I'd planned to do to it.

"But—"

"I made a deal. With Edward. Saving Ash gets me a pass, Haley too. But not you." I indicated the others. "Not them. So go."

I held his gaze; I knew better than to look away, and at last, he nodded. But right before he turned, he whispered, "You're everything I hold dear, Sunshine."

Then between two blinks, he became a wolf, and they all loped away, through parking lots and backyards where lights had begun to click on bit by bit.

"*Did* you make a deal?" Ash asked.

From the opposite direction that Gideon and the others had disappeared, well-armed men and women appeared—at least twenty, I didn't bother to count. They carried rifles, shotguns, some had pistols in holsters, several wore bandoliers of sparkling silver bullets. They pulled up at the sight of us, and every barrel seemed trained on me.

"No," I said.

Ash knocked me to the ground as gunfire erupted. Would the *Jager-Suchers* shoot him to get to me? I couldn't allow that. Unfortunately in this form, Ash was stronger, and when I struggled, he pressed me into the ground. But he didn't jerk, and he didn't gasp, and he didn't die.

Instead, a howl of pain was cut short by a burst, then a whoosh. I managed to turn my head in time to see Judas—too near to us for comfort—go up in flames. Guess he'd managed to gnaw off that leg after all. As he twisted and turned, the gargantuan wolf reformed into a slim, short, dying man.

Ash rolled off me and stood; he didn't offer a hand.

I gained my feet as Edward and his wife arrived, along with Haley. I was so glad to see her in one piece I almost hugged her. Would have, but she pulled off her bark-gray sweatshirt—she wore a tank top beneath as kids did now—and helped me into it. Her greater height meant the garment covered any areas I might not want revealed to old folks and strangers.

"Go," Edward ordered his pack of hunters. "They are getting away."

Concern for my wolves flared, but there was little I could do. I'd have to depend on Gideon to save them.

"You took long enough to blow shit up," I said, once the others had gone.

La Mémé set her hand on her husband's arm, which now cradled a rifle that appeared almost as ancient as he was. "There were complications."

"There are always complications." Edward's abundant white eyebrows drew together. "For instance, you, the newest luna werewolf. Were you going to tell me?"

"Oh, hell no."

His lips twitched.

"If you'd hit the boom button earlier," I continued, "you wouldn't know now."

"I always know. Eventually."

I rolled my eyes, and his amusement melted away. It would be better if he didn't know what he knew, if none of them did, and I could make that happen.

I set my fingers to my forehead. "I am not the luna werewolf."

Instead of Edward, his wife, Ash, even Haley repeating what I'd said and believing it, I felt a push back, same as I had in the cave when—

I looked at *La Mémé*. "You cast a spell."

"It is what a mambo does best."

"A mambo," I repeated. "A sorceress."

"If you like."

I did not like.

"Zane pulled this on me. His *grand-mère* was a mambo."

Edward and his wife exchanged a cryptic glance.

"Seems like a pretty big coincidence that you are too."

"*Oui*," *La Mémé* said.

Did that mean it was a coincidence or it wasn't?

"Enough of this." Edward slashed his hand, ending the conversation, at least for now. "Haley has spun a tale of nose bumps and peaceful werewolves without the insane urge to kill."

Ash snorted. "Grandfather, really?"

"Your grandmother convinced me to give her, to give them—or at least any of those that manage to escape tonight—the benefit of the doubt. For now."

Ash opened his mouth, and Edward lifted a finger. "We have

other fish to fry. Whether I believe her or not, the fact remains that before this magic nose bump, the wolves of these packs killed rampantly. The beta of one murdered my granddaughter, her son, and husband. He kidnapped Haley. They kidnapped others, kept them in cages like dogs, then sold them."

"That's over now, we—"

Edward shut me up with a look. "Because of what you did to save my grandson and protect my great-granddaughter, I will give you a chance to prove that you and yours are what you say you are and not just very, very good at hiding it."

"Okay." I could already see complications, but as the old man had said, there were always complications.

"One single disappearance, one blotch of unexplained blood in your territory, and I will come down on you like the Horsemen of the Apocalypse."

I doubted, even with his wife's magic stay-alive spell, that he would be riding any horses, Apocalyptic or otherwise, but I managed not to say so.

I wasn't going to be around to keep my territory in line since I still had the unsanctioned killing of Wendell hanging over my head. Of course if Zane died, that secret died with him. Something to think about.

But Gideon would do his best to pull the packs in line. Call it his mission.

Edward shouldered his rifle, then offered his arm to his wife. As they walked away, he frowned at the pile of ash and bone that had once been Jude Sicariot. "How are we going to explain away a missing rock star?"

"You will figure it out, *mon coeur*, you always do."

Ash brushed past me, paused, turned, and for an instant, I thought he might hold me, kiss me, at least thank me.

Such a fool.

"We're even now." The eyes I'd once compared to the flakes of gray death that fluttered in his wake hardened to banked coal. "I don't care what the old man promised; he's getting soft in the head."

I laughed. One thing Edward was not was soft.

"Next time I see you," Ash said, "I'll kill you."

My laughter died. "Next time."

A BAIT AND SWITCH

"He doesn't mean it, Luna." Haley stared after her uncle, her expression disconsolate.

I put my arm around her waist. "He does."

She set her cheek atop my head. "I know."

I tugged her close, hugged her hard—poor, motherless child. "Not your fault."

She pulled away. "Feels like it."

"Nope. This is Zane's fault." I indicated the newly mangled Camp Randall. "All of it."

"Okay."

"We should probably get out of here before the cops and the fire department find us."

I was surprised they hadn't already. The sirens had stopped on the other side of the structure, colored lights flared across the sky, and voices called out in the depths of the stadium's darkness.

"Wait," I said. "I thought the stadium was warded. That no one could hear or see any of this."

"Once the Hakim is gone, so is the spell."

I remembered the tall, bug-like shadow that had slipped into the night right before Gideon arrived, and the *bing, bing, bing* of lights going on in the surrounding buildings as if a ruckus had suddenly been heard. It hadn't hit me until now what that meant. I'd been a little busy.

"They'll be asking questions we don't wanna answer," Haley said.

"Like where are my pants?"

"Worse."

I could push them, but that was a lot of pushing, so as the shouts came closer, we hurried across the street. The area was packed with houses, apartments, taverns, restaurants, but it was Wisconsin, so there were also a lot of trees.

We ducked behind the trunk of a hefty maple as several police officers emerged from the stadium. The ashes of Judas fluttered above them, caught the breeze, and blew away.

They went back in, pausing at the pile of bones.

"Grandfather will explain this away. The bones. The stadium. Everything. You'll see."

"Why?"

"The less people trying to figure out a mystery, the less chance they'll stumble over an even bigger one."

"And get in his way."

"Or get dead."

That made a certain sort of sense. I had no doubt the news reports would say Camp Randall had suffered a gas leak, one dead, a few injuries. The place would be rebuilt bigger and better than before. Life goes on.

"I'm going to head to Jenna's apartment," I said. "I want you to find Gideon."

"No. You're my—"

"Luna. And I order you to warn him about Zane."

I'd meant to, would have, but I'd had to choose the most viable threat at the time—Edward and the rest his tribe.

"I think he knows."

"Does he?"

Uncertainty flickered. "Well, he knows Zane's a dick."

I choked, and she sent me a sheepish smile.

"Tell him the gladiator execution was a bait and switch."

"A bait and—"

"The lottery, the battles were the bait, a distraction. The switch? It was never about revenge on Ash—or not completely—it was a coup. Get everyone in one place, then take out the opposition."

"But Grandfather put a stop to it."

"You think Zane will stop?"

She sighed. "No. But can't you just call Alpha and explain?"

"It's better if he hears this in person." Because I needed to do a bait and switch myself—a.k.a. drop a buttload of lies, then disappear. "Wait for me in Shipwreck Bay."

Still, she hesitated.

I hadn't wanted to do this to the kid. It felt like I was taking advantage of her loyalty, but her loyalty was also the reason for it. She would not let me go. I had an instant to hope that *La Mémé's* magic blocking spell had left with her—otherwise I wasn't sure what I'd have done—before I lifted my fingers toward my forehead.

Haley's eyes widened, and she managed one step in my direction before I spoke. "Find Gideon and tell him what I said. All of it."

"Tell Alpha all of it," she repeated, and then she was gone.

As strutting down a sidewalk blazing with streetlights wearing a shirt but nothing else was gonna raise questions, especially with all that was going on nearby, I kept to the backyards, side streets, and shadows.

I didn't see any werewolf bodyguard as I approached Jenna's building. He or she had either gone to the rumble—which wouldn't be very bodyguard-ish—or they were very good at staying out of sight, which *was* very bodyguard-ish.

But no one stopped me from entering the building and

knocking on Jenna's door. Why would they? I was still the luna. For the time being.

The tiny woman who opened Jenna's door was in her late forties, maybe early fifties, wearing jeans and a chunky knit sweater the shade of St. Patrick's Day. She had short dark hair and big dark eyes that swept over my bare legs and bare feet before lifting to my own. "Your mom's here, Jenna."

"Mom!" Jenna threw back the door so hard it banged against the wall; she caught it on the rebound with the heel of her hand. "Where have you been? Why didn't you call?"

I'd tossed my phone out a window, planned to buy a burner, instead been kidnapped, then spent four days in a cave prison, been teleported to a blood-sport battle, and—

"Never mind that now." I urged her into the apartment and shut the door, threw the lock, attached the security chain.

The stranger folded her arms. "Not going to be much good against a werewolf."

I folded my arms too. "Mad scientist, I presume?"

"Mom!" Jenna's voice was mortified, but the mad scientist in question smiled. When she did, she looked a lot younger.

"You can call me Danny."

I turned to my daughter. "Got any pants?"

Laughter bubbled from Jenna's throat. "That's all you gotta say?"

"First things first."

Jenna disappeared into her room, came out with red UW sweatpants. I'd have to roll up the cuffs since Jenna had five inches on me but good enough.

I swayed as I drew them on, and Danny caught me. "You seem loopy. When was the last time you ate?"

I drew a blank.

"Picture it in your mind."

As soon as I did, I slapped my hand over my mouth and

sprinted for the toilet where I confirmed the last thing I'd eaten had been Judas.

Minutes that seemed like hours, maybe days, later, I lifted my head from the bowl, managed to gain my feet, wash my face, and rinse my mouth with mouthwash.

As soon as I turned off the faucet, I heard whispering in the hall and yanked open the door one of them had been thoughtful enough to close. I certainly hadn't had the wherewithal.

They stopped whispering and faced me, Jenna wide-eyed, Danny narrow.

"I gotta go, baby."

"You can't." Jenna grabbed my hand. "Tell her, Danny."

My skin prickled. "Tell me what?"

"Let's sit you down before you fall down."

Danny led the way into the living room where we took seats on the nicer than the usual college furniture Patrick had insisted upon—Jenna and I on the sofa, Danny on the moonlit-lake-blue wingback chair. She set her elbows on her knees and leaned in. "Here's the thing, Sarah. Werewolves don't get sick. Well, the virus, yes, but you had an injection."

"Yet sick I just was." And thought I might be again very soon.

"I need to do some tests."

"And I need to get gone." I looked at my daughter. "You know why."

"I do too," Danny said.

"Jenna!" The more people who knew the secret of dead Wendell, the less chance there was of keeping that secret.

"She can help."

"Help how?"

"Right now, by finding out what's happening with you."

My head had started to whirl again, worse than before. "Fine! Whatever." I made a shooing motion at Jenna. "I gotta lie down."

It was lucky I did since shortly thereafter, everything went dark.

More whispering greeted me as I came around. I sat up, got a major head rush.

I was still on the couch. I could see Dr. Danny in the kitchen fiddling with something on the counter. Glass *tinked* against glass, and I sniffed. "Why do I smell blood?"

Danny lifted her head, cast me a glance. "You said I could." She returned her attention to whatever she was doing with glass and blood.

"She took some samples." Jenna knelt and patted the fresh adhesive bandage stuck to the bend of my arm.

"I keep equipment in my car." Danny lifted a test tube filled with . . . yep, blood. Seemed like a lot of it. "I never knew when the alpha might call and want me . . ." She became too preoccupied with whatever she was doing to finish the sentence, so I finished it for her.

"To come running, which you would because the werewolves were—*are*—funding your research."

She ignored me, gaze riveted on whatever results she'd found in my blood. "You don't have the virus, but I didn't think you did."

I hadn't thought I did either. I'd felt the virus before Jenna had given me the injection; this was not it. I *had* felt like this before. When I'd picked up some bug from Jenna or at a political whatsit I hadn't wanted to attend.

"What does she have?" Jenna's voice wavered.

"Don't be scared." I squeezed her hand. "I'm not."

The flu, even one I wasn't supposed to have, was the least of my worries.

"This seems like . . .," Danny murmured. "Huh." She came into the living room and rooted around in a black doctor's bag on the floor, then pulled out a plastic cup and handed it to me. "Can you pee in that?"

"No." It wasn't that easy to hit the cup and not your hand.

"Just do it," Jenna said. "Please."

It wasn't pretty, but I managed.

The doctor took the sample and headed into the kitchen. Jenna and I stood awkwardly in the hall, uncertain if we should follow, stay where we were, or go watch TV.

A short while later, Danny said, "Huh," again.

"What. The. Hell?" I said louder than I needed to, but come on!

She lifted her gaze to mine. "You're pregnant."

"I am not!"

"She can't be," Jenna said.

"I went through premature menopause. Two years ago."

"But lycanthropy heals, Sarah."

"Gunshot and knife wounds not made with silver. Broken noses."

Danny shook her head. "Everything. Lycanthropy heals everything."

"But there's nothing wrong with me. Every woman goes through menopause."

"Not that early. It's not natural."

"Being a werewolf isn't natural!" I shouted.

"Calm down," Jenna said. "I know it's a shock, but it does solve the pack's problem."

Then it hit me. I'd thought Gideon had chosen me for love, despite what choosing me would cost him. But he'd known that I'd be healed. He'd known I'd get pregnant.

And Zane . . .

Oh shit. Zane. I suddenly understood so much.

"I will kill him," I said.

But which him?

The End

Are you ready for the conclusion of Sarah's story?

IN THE MIDNIGHT HOUR

A Midnight Madness Nightcreature Novel Book #3

IN THE MIDNIGHT HOUR

Just when I thought it was safe to go home...

I've been running too long. I'd gotten sloppy. Sloppy gets you captured. But it turns out, the very one I thought I had to hide from, saved me.

I just want to live peacefully. But happy family, er, *pack* reunions don't seem to be in my future. When my dark secret is used against me, I'm forced to run again. This time, help comes from the most unexpected source, the greatest werewolf hunter of all time, Edward Mandenauer.

To get what we both want—the end of the sadistic, yet sexy, werewolf Zane—Edward and I join forces. But Zane isn't working alone. Nor is he who or what he says he is. He's much, much more...

All I want is the life I believed I'd lost, but at this rate, I'll end up captured, imprisoned, enslaved . . . or dead.

From the voice of *New York Times* bestselling author Lori Handeland, the final installment in the *Midnight Madness* trilogy takes you deep into her Nightcreature world, complete with the humor, depth of characterization and fast-paced plot lines the author is known for while showcasing her incredible range.

IN THE MIDNIGHT HOUR

DEAR READER

Dear Reader,

All right, I blew up Camp Randall. Well, actually Edward did it so . . .

In all seriousness, Camp Randall is just fine. Right where I left it. All in one piece. But it was fun to play "What If . . .?" It's always fun to play "What If . . .?"

I hope you are enjoying the adventures of Sarah Sullivan and my foray into paranormal women's fiction with the "Midnight Madness" trilogy, loosely connected to my popular Nightcreature Novels.

Presently, there are eleven full length novels, two novellas and three short stories in the Nightcreature world, along with another spinoff trilogy, "Sisters of the Craft." A list of all my novels can be found on my website.

When the paranormal women's fiction genre came into being several years ago, a writer friend suggested I try my hand. Other commitments kept me from doing so right away, but when I did, Sarah was right there waiting for me—an older heroine, like me, ready for love and adventure.

Word-of-mouth can really help an author out, so if you enjoyed this book, I'd love it if you shared that with your friends.

In the same vein, reviews are critically important. If you're so inclined, I'd appreciate a Review (it can be as short as you'd like) on the platform where you purchased it. I would appreciate it very much!

I love hearing from my readers and can be contacted via my website (LoriHandeland.com), through Facebook (Lori Handeland Books) and on Instagram (Lori Handeland Books).

Subscribe to my NEWSLETTER for all the latest updates. Learn about new books, sales, and the occasional freebie.

I look forward to seeing you there!

Lori Handeland

ABOUT THE AUTHOR

Lori Handeland is a five-time nominee and two-time winner of the prestigious RITA™ Award from Romance Writers of America, as well as the New York Times and USA Today bestselling author of over sixty novels spanning the genres of paranormal romance, urban fantasy, contemporary romance, historical romance, historical fantasy and women's fiction. Her novel *Just Once* received a coveted, starred review from Library Journal and was optioned as a feature film by Catalyst Global Media.

Lori lives in Southern Wisconsin with her husband of over thirty-five years. In between writing and reading, she enjoys long walks with their rescue mutt, Arnold, and visits from her two grown sons, awesome daughter-in-law and perfectly adorable grandchildren.

MORE BOOKS BY LORI?

I have written over sixty novels, novellas and short stories across multiple genres. But whether you read a contemporary or a historical, a women's fiction or a paranormal, you will always find my signature voice, along with a little humor, a little angst and the depth of characterization and fast-paced plot lines I love to read as well as write.

You can download a complete LIST of my novels on my website.

COPYRIGHT

Blame it on Midnight

Cover Art The Killion Group, Inc.

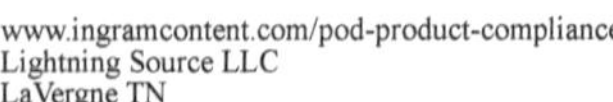
www.ingramcontent.com/pod-product-compliance
Lightning Source LLC
LaVergne TN
LVHW020648100826
845148LV00012B/2371

* 9 7 9 8 9 8 8 0 0 2 3 4 5 *